THE TRAITORS' GATE:

A CHRONICLE OF OLD LONDON.

EXECUTION OF MARY, QUEEN OF SCOTS.

CHAPTER I.

THE MARTYRED CORPSE.

SHOWING HOW CHIDIOCK TITCHBOURNE CAME TO LONDON TO AID IN THE CONSPIRACY—HOW HE SAW THE CORPSE OF RICHARD HUNNE BURNT AT WESTMINSTER, AND OF THE ADVEN-TURE WHICH BEFEL HIM.

TOWARDS the latter end of October, 1586, a strange scene took place in the churchyard of Westminster Abbey.

A scene, whose horrible accompaniments fixed it in the memories of those who witnessed it long after it had passed away.

The *dead body* of Richard Hunne, citizen of London, and inhabitant of the parish of Saint Martin's-in-the-Fields, court tailor by profession, but a proven spy of the Papists, was about to be burnt, and though the execution of the sentence followed almost immediately upon its promulgation, a great crowd had assembled to witness it.

Among the mass of people were two men who will figure largely in our history.

The foremost of these was a tall, handsome youth of some twenty summers, who was evidently no stranger to the Sanctuary of Westminster.

He was ragged and rustic in appearance, and looked like one of the rural or vagabond population, who in the previous reign of Mary would have had free access to any monastery, for, as a rule, they were devoted to the monks, from whom they received many benefits.

He was looked at by the crowd, which was mainly composed of Puritans and new Reformers, with evident distrust and suspicion.

The other was a man in a very shabby suit of legal robes, who was watching the scene with interest, and who seemed struck with the ingenious horror depicted upon the countenance of the youth by his side.

Facing the north gate of the abbey, on the opposite side of the churchyard, was the Gatehouse Prison.

It was a massive, square built tower, over a deep archway, which gave admittance into the Sanctuary of Westminster; the entrance to this was defended by a raised portcullis which was called in those days Jonah's jaws.

Between the Abbey and this prison to the west of Saint Margaret's Chapel was a space of a circular form, with a huge granite stone in the centre.

This was known as the Place of Ordeal, and was distinguished by a tall stake some ten feet high, set in a socket hollowed in the judgment stone.

Around this were piles of faggots and shavings, while a cask of pitch stood near at hand to heighten the flames.

A guard of armed yeoman and halberdiers surrounded the stake.

The bailiff of Westminster, a man of knightly rank, in whose family the office was hereditary, with the assistance of the attendants and some dozen or so eager Protestants among the crowd to clear a space between the Abbey and the Gatehouse.

As soon as this was effected the joy bells of the Abbey began to ring merrily.

Almost at the same instant the processions emerged, one from the prison, the other from the church.

The former carried in its ranks the condemned corpse, stretched on a bier, surrounded by the javelin men who were attached to the bailiwick of Westminster.

The latter consisted altogether of Puritan preachers.

As the bier, covered by a piece of black pitch cloth, from which a boot projected in one direction, and a motionless purple hand in the other, alone giving warning that the corpse of a human being lay beneath came in view, the rabble shouted—

"The Papist, the Papist spy."

"Death to the Papist."

"Smite the abominations of the scarlet woman."

"Faggot and flare for the adherents of the accursed Pope."

"To the stake with the corpse."

"Canst thou tell the meaning of this strange scene, good master?" asked the shabbily-dressed youth of the seedy-garbed man of law.

"Aye, worthy youth, that can I right well," replied the lawyer. "The body that thou seeest on yonder bier was that of a friend of mine own—once Richard Hunne—a good man and worthy citizen, who hath grievously offended the straight-laced followers of the thrice-accursed Martin Luther by his strict adherence to the religion of his forefathers. So, perforce, they dub him a Papist spy and cast him into prison; but, while he awaits his trial, Lo! he either puts an end to his own existence or is privately destroyed by those who have him in charge, for some base purpose of their own."

The last words were spoken in so low a tone that they reached the ears of no one but the youth to whom they were addressed.

"Yes," continued the lawyer, still speaking in a low tone, "Hunne was discovered hanging in his cell in the Gatehouse Prison which belongs to the Abbey; but I have been told that he was not merely strangled, but that his neck was broken, and that marks of foul play were visible upon his person. Now, forsooth, the Protestants would have us believe that the Devil came into Hunne's cell, all fire and flame, and strangled him, so that my unfortunate friend should attend and sing the *Salve* at the witches next Sabbath revel. But come, let's push nearer to the stake, good rural," he went on; "we'll get as near to the body as we can, for I long, above all things, to verify whether the poor man's neck is broken by murder or the devil, or simply twisted by his own exertions. Being from the country, as thy appearance showeth, thou art doubtless well skilled in the strangling of poultry, and may give me thy judgment on this fowl of Diogenes, who has been as much sacrificed as the unfortunate white cock of the Jews.

Thus saying, the lawyer, followed by his companion, forced his way through the closely packed crowd.

At this moment, one of the Protestant Bishops prepared to ascend the stone on the Place of Ordeal, to perform the customary ceremony of declaring the heresies and crimes of the condemned, before delivering the body of Richard Hunne to the secular powers.

The Bishop, who stood before the huge assembly, was of low stature, lean and sinewy, and distinguished by a peculiar writhing motion, caused by the ominous addition of a club-foot, a deformity which popular inauguration identified as an infallible characteristic of the Prince of Darkness himself.

His head was disproportionately large, and his physiognomy combined some singular and startling incongruities.

A forehead of great intellectual expansion could not conceal the unfavourable effect of the lower visage, which was coarse and sensual to a degree.

Satyr and demi-god seemed united in its expression.

"Who is yonder man?" asked the youth.

"Thou are a rural—and knoweth not I readily perceive," was the lawyer's reply. "There are but few in Westminster who know not that renegade— the apostate from the Holy Catholic religion, Iscariot; he was the first to embrace the new doctrines, and to follow that Dragon of Heresy, Martin Luther, to the shame of all good men be it said. The Protestants have made him a Bishop, and to make the sad story still more disgraceful," went on the speaker, "In the reign of good Queen Mary, he was the most ascetic conventual in the whole monastery, and was like to have succeeded the aged Abbot Felip, had not this sudden change come about. But cease thy questions, I pray thee, for see, the thrice-accursed wretch is about to speak."

The renegade Benedictine waited, with his eyes fixed in sombre humility upon the ground, until the tumult made on the appearance of Hunne's body, and the murmur of anger which greeted his own appearance, had gradually subsided.

"Masters and friends," began the orator, *Sancta Obedientia*, I am here to obey the call, and fight in the cause of the Most High, and to declare to you for what cause the miserable carcase of Richard Hunne is this day to be delivered to the flames. His soul is already plunged into the unquenchable fire of Hell to answer of Papistical opinions, and Jesuitical plots against the peace of this realm; and

the Protestant Faith which corrupted men's consciences far more than his lifeless body now taints the air the foul stench which arises from it. For the few words that I am about to speak," went on the *ci devant* monk, "I will give you a text, *Est blasphemia in castris*. There is blasphemy in the camp, not only blasphemy, but idolatory; and well may I say so, for hath not the fallacies of Rome spanned upon the earth, have not even I been one of their many victims, had I not battled fiercely with the Popish fiend, and resolutely tore myself away. Here at my feet lays the corpse of another of the victims of the woman of Babylon. This Richard Hunne was a potent and pestilent papist, who would gladly have raised the banner of Rome, and have renewed the days of Bloody Mary amongst us; these accusations have been proven against him, and his body is justly condemned to the flames.

"I cry you mercy, good Bishop," interrupted a voice at this moment, and to the surprise and admiration of the youth, his companion, the lawyer, stepped boldly forward, and challenged attention. "I cry you mercy, but I must enter a protest on behalf of this silent defendant at your feet, and to tell thee plainly to thy face, that if the Puritans wouldst prove their innocence of the blood guiltiness laid to their charges, ye take an ill way to muffle the corpse thus from the sight of all men, and to propose its utter consumings as if thereby ye could hide it from God's sight also."

During this speech the apostate Iscariot had remained petrified with astonishment, then with crimson visage, he suddenly recovered himself.

"Ah! I recognise thee, Ballard, in spite of this disguise," thundered forth Iscariot, "Mind, false Papist, that thou sharest not the same fate as hath thy friend and confederate, Richard Hunne. But come, ye Lutherans, put forth without the gates this daring monk, who steals like a wolf concealed beneath a sheepskin amongst you, seeking whom he may devour."

At the mention of Ballard's name the youth gave a start, and laid his hand on that of the lawyer, or rather monk—who for some purpose of his own had assumed that attire.

But, ere he could speak, the decree of Iscariot was being put into execution—and in the roughest manner.

A mob, consisting of the most ferocious reprobates of the Sanctuary, rushed upon the bold monk, who made an energetic but useless resistance for some instants, during which the country youth was thrown down and trampled upon.

When he arose again he perceived that Ballard had been thrust outside the Abbey gates, amidst a savage, shouting multitude, who covered him with blows and mud.

The voice of the audacious monk was lost in the uproar, but his gestures still evinced defiance, and he shook his clenched fist at Iscariot as he was hurled out.

The Puritan looked on calmly, with folded arms and a smile of withering contempt, but rather, as it seemed to the youth, at the executants of his will than at his antagonists.

He then proceeded with the interrupted ceremonial, as if nought had occurred to disturb the order of the proceedings, and read the sentence on Richard Hunne, and the long list of signatures that followed the decrees, with emphatic slowness, concluding with the formulæ of delivering the body to the secular powers, to be dealt with according to the law.

And it was with relentless emphasis that he pronounced the words of the curse, sealing the excommunication of a Papist—

"𝔄𝔫𝔡 𝔪𝔞𝔶 𝔥𝔦𝔰 𝔰𝔬𝔲𝔩, 𝔩𝔦𝔨𝔢 𝔥𝔦𝔰 𝔟𝔬𝔡𝔶, 𝔠𝔬𝔫𝔰𝔲𝔪𝔢, 𝔟𝔲𝔯𝔫, 𝔞𝔫𝔡 𝔰𝔱𝔦𝔫𝔨 𝔦𝔫 𝔢𝔟𝔢𝔯𝔩𝔞𝔰𝔱𝔦𝔫𝔤 𝔣𝔩𝔞𝔪𝔢𝔰; 𝔞𝔪𝔢𝔫."

Then Iscariot turned to the high bailiff, and, indicating the muffled victim at his feet, murmured in a low tone—

𝔍𝔫 𝔫𝔬𝔪𝔦𝔫𝔢 𝔇𝔬𝔪𝔦𝔫𝔦; 𝔞𝔪𝔢𝔫.

He then descended from the Stone of the Ordeal; but, as his feet touched the ground, he gave a low moan of horror, and staggered back, at the same time drawing his mantle tightly around him.

It was a terrible sight that had thus affected the Puritan.

A stream of dark liquid had oozed from the already corrupted carcase, and was slowly running towards his feet.

With a shudder, with averted eyes and blanched features, he avoided it, and glided away through the opening masses of the populace, who made a general movement towards the stake.

The bailiff's men now raised the bier, the pitch-cloth was removed, and the body of Richard Hunne was exposed to view, festering and rotting in the garment which it had worn during life.

The furred gown and golden chain of an honorable guild still remained upon him; but all speculations as to the state of his neck, whether fractured or twisted, was prevented by the fact that the girdle on which he had been found hanging had been bound round the dead man's neck so tightly that it was rigid, even when the attendants raised the body.

The youth, who was transfixed with the horrible scene, averted his eyes from the fearful and ghastly countenance, already far advanced towards decomposition, and looked in another direction.

Then was he fascinated by a look darted upon him from beneath the shade of a Puritan's hat, in the distance.

He perceived that the eyes of Iscariot were fixed upon him with a vague, unfathomable, and terrible expression.

The next moment, however, the Puritan disappeared beneath the arch of Solomon's Porch, followed by the rest of the clergy.

The body of Richard Hunne had by this time been lifted from the bier to the stake, chained to it, the faggots piled round, and, amid a shout of universal triumph from the Puritanical portion of the mob, fired.

Smoke and flame speedily obscured all view of the corpse, yet the youth continued to fix his horror-fascinated eyes upon it, until a chance waft of air suddenly gave him a last view of the consuming victim.

And then, either his imagination worked an hallucination on his strained vision, or else he saw that the girdle twisted round Hunne's neck being burst away, the neck had fallen brokenly on his chest, so that it seemed evident that the spine was fractured.

But again the smoke and flame enveloped the martyred corpse, and, in a few minutes, nought remains save a heap of black dust, piled circularly round the Stone of the Ordeal.

As the youth was about to turn away, he was accosted by a serving man.

"Are you from Southampton?" he asked.

The youth replied in the affirmative.

"Chidiock Titchbourne by name?"

"Yes."

"Then, sir, my master, Anthony Babington, and others are waiting your arrival."

"Good," replied the youth who had been called Chidiock Titchbourne; "lead on, I'll follow thee."

———

CHAPTER II.

THE SECRET CLUB IN RED LION COURT.—HOW CHIDIOCK TICHBOURNE MET THE CONSPIRATORS AT THE OLD CITY TAVERN, OF THE AR-

RANGEMENTS THAT WERE MADE TO SEIZE THE PERSON OF THE QUEEN, AND OF THE SUDDEN MANNER IN WHICH ANTHONY BABINGTON AND HIS ASSOCIATES WERE BETRAYED.

IN the year 1586, few fields and green lanes separated the village of Charing from the city.

Midway between Westminster and Charing stood the Cross of Charing, a handsome monument which had been raised to the memory of Queen Eleanor, and which the zeal of the reformers had greatly defaced.

Hard by, was the gothic chapel and hermitage of Saint Catherine, now in ruins—only a few mouldering fragments remaining to show the place where it had once proudly stood.

These buildings were directly opposite the ancient Cross of Charing, but the space between them, which had once been a smooth lawn, with flowering shrubs, had been neglected for many years.

Long rank grass had sprung up.

Thistles, nightshades, ground ivy and briony, had grown luxuriantly amidst the ruins.

Nought remained of the chapel save its graceful Norman Arch.

Doors had been torn from their hinges, and the sculptured form of Saint Catherine, which had originally adorned the exterior, had been destroyed in the rage and savage fury against the Catholics.

The very altar had been crushed into fragments, and in that desecrated chapel, where the melodious chant of devotion had once been heard, no sound disturbed the stillness but the hollow sighing of the wind, and the weird screaming of the gloomy owl.

As Chidiock Titchbourne passed the once hallowed spot with his companion, he reverently raised his cap, and with a vow of hatred against the persecutors of his religion, pursued his course down the Strand.

A fair spot it was, with the mansions of the nobles and the green slope which stretched down to the verge of the river.

Here was York House, and near the site of the present Railway Station at Charing Cross, the ancient palace of the Savoy; and a little further on the palace of the Protector Somerset, which had been built from the ruins of the beautiful cloisters of the cathedral of Saint Paul, which had been pulled down for that purpose; while the bones of those who rested there were dug up, and thrown into Finsbury Fields.

Entering the precincts of the City of London, Titchbourne and the serving man turned up a narrow passage in Fleet Street, which is now known as Red Lion Court.

In this court, and upon the site of our publishing office, there was situated in the reign of Queen Elizabeth, a smoke-dried, dingy looking tavern, whose inn sign indicated it to be "The Lion with the Opened Mouth."

It was towards this hostelrie that the two men advanced.

On this October day, various groups of men might have been noticed making their way towards this dim and obscure tavern.

Men in almost every variety of attire, who one by one had shrunk into the narrow doorway, and had confronted a sour visaged host, who received them with a whispered word and a significant gesture.

Silently and noiselessly—but for the whispered word and gesture, they passed in, one by one.

Evidently they all knew their way, for without any further greeting, they proceeded to a large room upon the first floor, where even through the carefully closed shutter, a twinkle of light could be discerned from the exterior.

But ere one man was admitted, these were extinguished.

In the dark, and between two of the number appointed as sentries, as in a masonic lodge, each man entered, whispering the pass word of the evening.

As they did so, a black mask was given to each, with which they concealed their features.

When the twenty-five men, including Chidiock Titchbourne and his companion, who formed the assembly, had entered, the door was closed and securely fastened, and by some ingenious contrivance, twenty-five wax lights broke out in stars.

This was a signal that the club had opened.

The most remarkable sign of the dangerous character of the meeting, was the mysterious silence which was preserved not only in the room, but throughout the entire premises.

There were none of the usual tavern tumults.

Fretful bells were not clashing in noisy discord from a dozen rooms at once.

There was no important host—or good-humoured drawer bawling out with leather lungs——

"Score a flask of rhenish in the oaken room."

"Pipes and a bowl of punch in the blue parlour."

No swashbucklers reeling up and down the broad old-fashioned staircases.

No smack of kissing buxom damsels behind the door.

No scuffle or stamp of duellists' feet.

No glasses breaking—or oaths—or loud laughter.

Nothing but the dead oppressive silence, alone broken by the slow tramp of the corporation watchman in that city court.

To those acquainted with the plans of the conspirators, such as those now assembled, it would have been self-evident that scouts had been placed on every side to give notice of approaching danger.

There was a sentinel upon the high roof, with a small signal to communicate with the opposite side of the river.

There was a picket round the court.

In every quiet nook of the labyrinth of courts which ran between Fetter Lane and Gough Square, from Gough Square to Ludgate, there lurked a spy, in the pay of the mysterious confederation, which sat in solemn conclave at the "Lion with the Opened Mouth."

No horseman, or spy could steal upon them without detection.

The conspirators, the band of brothers, who had joined Anthony Babington in the conspiracy against Protestant Elizabeth, and who had sworn to place Mary Queen of Scots upon the British throne, sat like spiders.

They represented the centre of a net work of outposts, and from afar off, the sightest pulsation of danger would be conveyed to them.

The men who were here assembled, were desperate and wary patriots, not traitors, who fought for their rightful queen, and their true religion.

The most conspicuous object in the room, was a tall oak chair, with the black twisted back and the cane crossbars, so common in old houses.

This was occupied by the president of the club—Anthony Babington, of Dethic, in the County of Derby.

He was a young man with handsome but voluptuous features.

He was the only one in the apartment who did not wear a mask.

His attire was magnificent.

His doublet was of black velvet, puffed with gold tissue, nor were his limbs deformed by the enormous trunk hose so commonly worn at this time; his stockings were of knitted silk—then an article of great expense.

Large crimson rosettes decorated his shoes, and upon the small black velvet cap, which sat lightly on his head, was a plume of white feathers fastened by an agraffe of diamonds.

From his shoulders depended a mantle of scarlet cloth, richly embroidered with gold.

This article was particularly appropriated to the noblemen and gentlemen of the period.

A small falling ruffle of the finest foreign lace was left open at his throat, and the hilt of his rapier glittered with jewels.

Near to him was a man in the costume of an officer of halberdiers, who was addressed as Captain Fortescue, but with whom Chidiock Titchbourne had a vivid recollection of having met before.

A moment's consideration, aided by the tone of the officer, assured him that he was correct.

In him Chidiock recognised his legal friend of the morning—the man who had been thrust out of the Abbey gate—the Jesuit Priest, Ballard.

And now, at a signal given by three shrill and peculiar notes upon a whistle, the doors of the apartment flew open, and the sour, villianous-looking landlord, followed by a still more rascally and suicidal waiter, with long greasy hair and red-rimmed eyes, entered.

This man bore in a baked pike with a gudgeon fastened firmly between the teeth of that river shark.

None of the conspirators present were ignorant that those fish were emblemetical of the tyranny so soon to be levelled with the dust.

A low cheer broke forth from every throat.

But Babington instantly suppressed it by a wave of his right hand.

Standing up, the chief conspirator looked round each side of the room; then placing to his lips a small crucifix, which he fervently kissed, he bowed to the East, to the West, and to the South.

Laying aside the emblem of Christianity, he then took a silver whistle from his girdle, upon which he blew thrice.

As the third sound died away the twenty-five men who composed the assembly sprang to their feet with one accord.

Each man removed his hat and waved his sword high above his head.

Ere the crash of the returning blades had died away Ballard, or rather Captain Fortescue—as it was by this title that he was more generally known —took up a huge axe-like knife which lay upon the table beside him, and skilfully separating the flesh of the pike from the bones, divided it into twenty-five pieces.

He then passed a piece round to each man, having first splashed it with red wine.

This proceeding was meant to typify the Royal blood which these men were banded together to shed.

"Brethren," cried Babington in a commanding voice, "the hour, the day for which we have so patiently watched and waited has at length arrived. Our wrongs—the wrongs and indignities which have been heaped upon the head of our persecuted Queen, shall now be avenged, and Mary Stuart, the blood-royal descendant of Henry VII.— a married Queen of France and the anointed Queen of Scotland—shall have her own again."

A low murmur of loyalty broke forth.

"All arrangements have been made," went on Babington, "and the attack will take place ere to-morrow's sun shall have set."

"We have received instructions," interposed Ballard, "that now lying off Dover are the Spanish men-of-war, crowded with soldiers, who but await our convenience to hasten to our assistance."

"My retainers are armed and even now on their way to London," broke in Chidiock Titchbourne; "ere long they will arrive to lift their brawny Hampshire arms in so good a cause."

"That is well," said John Savage, a man of desperate courage, who had served some years in the Low Countries under the Prince of Parma, "and, in addition to that, we have the tenants and peasantry of Edward Windsor, Thomas Salisbury, Robert Gage, John Traveres, John Jones, Henry Donne, and Charles Tilner."

"The priests Maude and Gifford, from the English Seminary at Rheims," said Babington, reading from a paper, "have gleaned many important particulars relating to the movements of Elizabeth's government. The Jesuit Gifford has, by bribing the servants at Tutbury Castle, obtained an interview with our Queen, who, as you are well aware, is confined there under the charge of Sir Amias Paulet. To her he showed the sketch, containing portraits of the five and twenty here assembled, which sketch was drawn at her desire by myself. Her Majesty," continued Babington, mentioning the title of his Queen in a tone of respectful admiration, "Her Majesty had been pleased to approve of our designs, and further mentions that those who remain faithful to her interest, may expect all the rewards that it will be in her power to confer."

"What says the Queen with reference to our intention regarding Elizabeth," queried Charnoe, one of the conspirators, and a wealthy gentleman of Lancashire?"

"That the death of Elizabeth is a necessary circumstance, before any attempt is made either for her own deliverance, or for insurrection," rejoined Babington.

"Good then, let us lose no further time in execution of the project," cried Savage, bringing his hand heavily down upon the table.

"Let us not rush upon the question in this hasty manner, friend Savage," said Ballard, "you are too eager, and require a dose of alembroth to temper thy blood."

"Ballard is correct," went on Babington, "one fatal move would bring ruin and death to all of us—no, we must proceed with the utmost caution, for Nau and Curle, the private secretaries of Queen Mary, have forwarded to the care of myself and our brother Ballard, a packet of papers and correspondence which will greatly aid us in our designs. I have also letters from the Queen to Mendoza, the Spanish Ambassador, at the Court of France, to Charles Paget, the Archbishop of Glasgow, and to Sir Francis Inglefield."

As Babington concluded, he drew from his doublet a packet of papers which he laid before him.

"Hold!" cried Captain Abington, one of the conspirators, whose father had been cofferer to the household of Queen Elizabeth, "Hold, before you proceed further; here is a new member to be elected, one who has suffered much for the cause."

All eyes were turned upon the man who proposed to join the company, as he was pointed out by the old red-faced Captain.

The proposed new member seemed an old, bent-up man, with long, wavy white hair, covered by a greasy skull cap which came down over his ears.

"Who will vouch for the fidelity of our new brother," demanded Ballard in a hoarse, suspicious tone.

"That can I, right willingly!" shouted Abington, with animation. 'Fore heaven, gentlemen, didn't he lose both his ears in the pillory under the infernal Act of Parliament passed against the Catholics in 1584, and haven't five of his sons been brought to the scaffold through their adherence to their Queen and their religion? He's too old now for the firelock, but he can hold forth on a tub as well as the best of you."

"Enough! enough!" cried a dozen voices;

"Like us he has suffered—like us he shall have vengeance."

As the cry was raised, the old gentleman changed his seat, as if with the object of obtaining a better place of hearing, and sat down exactly opposite the packet of documents which Anthony Babington had placed upon the table.

"This sacred packet," went on Anthony Babington, "must be guarded with our lives. The secrets which are contained therein will cause such a revolution in this kingdom that have never before been witnessed. Ha! am I speaking to dogs or wolves?" he suddenly shouted, looking fiercely round as a hubbub of voices arose, and one or two of the more incredulous hands were thrust in the direction of the packet.

"One inch nearer," cried Ballard, springing back a step and whirling his sword with a whistle round his head, "and, by Heaven, I'll lop off every hand that touches it."

The hands fell back and the fretting crowd resumed their seats.

"What means this distrust?" asked Babington, "in due time ye shall know the contents of these papers. The present moment is not the time for doubt. Recollect our motto—'Fidelity, Forbearance. and Faith.'"

"True, true."

The tide of favour was now with the speaker.

The eyes grew brighter, and congratulatory whispers were exchanged between the members.

"All goes well," went on Babington, "we all assemble at Ludgate to-morrow at three o'clock, when Elizabeth goes to the Guildhall. It is arranged that at the same time the flames shall break out in the provinces."

A low, hoarse, deep shout arose, but it was immediately repressed lest it should reach curious ears without.

"Our posts! our posts!" cried the new member with tottering feebleness, evidently overcome by the enthusiasm of the moment; "Let us slay the tyrant queen even while she sleeps."

"Moderate your zeal," returned Babington, as the old man fell back exhausted in his seat. "The work that is to be done is not for such as you, it must be executed by stronger arms and stronger heads."

Then. turning to one of the conspirators, he went on—

"To you, Charles Tinley, is assigned the honourable task of arresting the person of the Queen as she sets forth in her carriage for the City. You will be accompanied by a hundred of the men belonging to your division, heavily armed with sword, pistol, and arquebuse."

With a significant smile, Charles Tinley, a red-faced white hand of Cheshire cockfighter, touched the hilt of his sword with a gesture of deep meaning.

"To you, Captain Barnwell, devolves the honourable task of forcing an entrance into the Tower and securing that fortress."

Then, turning to Chidiock Titchbourne, he said—

"To you will be entrusted the onerous duty of securing the person of the Lord Mayor and preventing the calling out of the City trained bands. And now, gentlemen, let us have one bowl of punch and then to horse."

As he spoke the door opened, and the same host again entered, staggering beneath the weight of a smoking china bowl of punch, which he placed upon the table and then withdrew.

"With regard to these papers," said Ballard, "I will take charge of them; and while in my possession, let me see the one who will dare wrest them from me."

"I DARE," said the old man next to him, suddenly tearing off his white wig and disclosing the features of the renegade priest, Iscariot; and as he spoke he possessed himself of the packet of documents ere a hand of the astonished traitors could draw a sword to punish his temerity.

But the moment's silence soon broke into a storm of discordant noises and shouts, as the conspirators cried out in fierce anger and astonished rage—

"Kill the spy!"

"Down with the turncoat priest!"

"Hew him to pieces——"

"Burn him!"

"Limb him!"

"Slash him into mincemeat!"

Ere these threats could be put into execution Iscariot drew a pistol from his pocket and fired at the lock of the door, which split into a thousand fragments.

The next instant a mob of redcoats poured into the room.

Oaths, curses, and deep shouts of vengeance now filled the air.

The dreadful confusion was increased by the smoke and explosion of a hand grenade which one of the soldiers had thrown into the room.

Swords crossing and snapping.

Pistols firing—

Groans and curses—

Tables falling—windows breaking—

The whole place turned into a terrible scene of bloodshed and confusion.

Chidiock Titchbourne was engaged in attacking Iscariot, with the intention of recovering the papers.

But the recreant priest had the best of it.

Chidiock was hardly pressed.

Iscariot had beaten him down upon one knee.

His rapier was hurled from his grasp—

He felt that his last hour had arrived.

Closing his eyes, he awaited the final thrust of his adversary.

Suddenly the wainscoting of the room seemed to give way behind him—a sliding panel opened—and he was suddenly dragged through the wall, at the same moment that the sword of Iscariot descended.

——

CHAPTER III.

IMPRISONED IN THE TOWER OF LONDON.—SHOWING HOW BABINGTON AND CHIDIOCK TITCHBOURNE WERE ARRESTED IN FLEET STREET, OF THE MANNER IN WHICH THEY PASSED THROUGH TRAITORS' GATE, AND HOW THEY PARTED TO MEET NO MORE IN THIS WORLD.

CHIDIOCK TITCHBOURNE felt his arm closely grasped by his companion, whom he recognised by the voice to be Anthony Babington, for it was impossible to see in the intense darkness which reigned in the narrow secret passage, which they were traversing.

"Hush for your life," hoarsely whispered Babington. "Not a word. This passage will enable us to escape into Fleet Street, and you must at once away to Tutbury Castle, to the Queen, for I much fear me that, for the present, the conspiracy has received its deathblow."

"Alas, I fear so," replied Titchbourne, "but I will lose no time."

Closely following Anthony Babington, Titchbourne came at length to a small bolted door.

Rapidly unfastening this door, which led into a blind court off Fleet Street, Babington threw it open, but at the same instant a sight met his eyes that caused him to seize hold of Titchbourne, and endeavour to retreat.

But it was too late, the narrow passage was filled by a small band of soldiers fully accoutred in corselets and morions, and armed with swords, half pikes, and calivers.

At their head was a pursuivant.

"Hold," cried the pursuivant, in a loud voice. "In the name of her Most Gracious Majesty, Queen Elizabeth, I arrest you, Anthony Babington, and Chidiock Titchbourne, as traitors to your country;" then turning to a person who had hitherto remained concealed in an angle of the passage, the officer went on, "These are those for whom we are watching?"

"They are the Papist Plotters," replied the person questioned, coming forward, and revealing the sardonic features of Iscariot.

"Betrayed," cried Babington, springing back and drawing his sword, an example that was immediately followed by Titchbourne.

"Yes, betrayed if you will have it so," answered Iscariot, in a menacing tone. "Betrayed to the torture chamber, and the scaffold."

"You shall not live to boast of your infamy," shouted Titchbourne, shortening his weapon, and making a sudden thrust at Iscariot.

The recreant priest did not attempt to avoid the blow, on the contrary, he opened his breast to it.

The point of the sword pierced his doublet, and then with a sudden bound broke in twain.

"Behold, it is thus the Lord protects the anointed ministers of the true religion," he replied, sanctimoniously, hastily drawing the rent which the sword had made over the glittering coat of mail, which he wore beneath his outward garments.

And now the soldiers advanced upon the devoted catholics. Retreat was impossible, a short but desperate scuffle, angry shouts, and loud patter, and the two gentlemen were disarmed and prisoners.

"There'll be a goodly crew in the Tower of London, this night," said the pursuivant, grimly."

"And ample work for the sworn torturer, and the Headsman," brutally laughed one of the soldiers.

"Whither do you take us," demanded Titchbourne, as the party made their way through Alastia, or Whitefriars, as it is now known, in the direction of the river.

"To TRAITORS' GATE," sternly replied the officer.

Off the old landing stairs of Whitefriars, lay the pursuivants barge, and in this were the prisoners placed.

Scarcely were they seated, than the officer gave the signal to the rowers.

Two halberdiers, with torches, were placed in the forepart of the boat, which left a long track of light as it pursued its rapid course down the river.

The tide was in their favour, and they speedily shot old London Bridge, which was covered with outhouses, the noise of the falling water, and the mills falling dismally upon their ears.

And now the next object upon which their gaze rested, was the Tower.

And what food for reflection the sight of the ancient palace, prison, and fortress, gave the prisoners, as they approached the frowning yet picturesque building.

In the middle of the sixteenth century, the outer ramparts of the Tower were strongly fortified.

The gleam of corselet and pike were reflected upon the dark waters of its moat.

The inner walls were entire and unbroken, and thirteen towers reared their embattled fronts. In each of these towers were state prisoners immured. Its drawbridges were constantly raised, and its gates closed.

Within its precincts lodged Queen Elizabeth, and councils where held in its chambers.

Its secret dungeons were crowded, and a scaffold reared its head upon Tower Hill, the soil of which was dyed with the richest and best blood in the land.

Amongst its inferior officers, it numbered gaolers, sworn torturers, a prison chirurgeon, and a headsman, for all the terrible machinery was in readiness, and could be called into action at a moment's notice.

The steps of TRAITORS' GATE were worn by the feet of those who ascended them, and each structure of the gigantic building had dark and terrible secrets to conceal ; for, beneath all those ramparts, towers, and bulwarks, were subterranean passages and secret dungeons.

Striving to banish the gloomy reflections which, in spite of their efforts, obtruded themselves upon their minds, the two conspirators strained their gaze to discover through the gloom the White Tower, but they could discern nothing but a sombre mass, like a thunder cloud.

Saint Thomas's, or Traitors' Tower, was, however, plainly distinguishable, as several armed men carrying flambeaux were stationed on its summit.

The barge was now challenged by the sentinels, and almost before the answer could be returned by those on board, a wicket composed of immense beams of wood was opened, and the boat shot beneath the gloomy arch.

They had now passed Traitors' Gate.

Never had either Babington or Titchbourne experienced such feelings of horror as now assailed them.

Had they been crossing the fabled Styx, with the terrible Charon, the ferryman of Hell for their guide, they could not have felt greater dread.

Their blood seemed congealed in their veins.

The lurid light of the torches fell upon the black, dismal arch, upon the slimy walls, and upon the murky tide.

Nothing was heard but the ripple of the water, for the men had ceased rowing, and the barge, impelled by their former efforts, soon grated against the steps.

The shock recalled both Babington and Titchbourne to consciousness.

Several armed figures, bearing torches, now descended the steps.

Foremost among them was Sir Henry Bedingfield, the Constable of the Tower, surrounded by a number of the warders of the Tower.

The customary ceremony of delivering the warrant and receiving an acknowledgment for the bodies of the prisoners was then gone through, and the pursuivant requested the prisoners to disembark.

They were assisted to land by the warders.

"What, ho, warders !" cried the Constable of the Tower, addressing some of the men who stood by his side ; "conduct the traitor, Anthony Babington, to the dungeon prepared for him beneath the Devilin Tower, and Master Chidiock Titchbourne to the Beauchamp Tower, without delay."

"Are we, then, to be separated in our captivity ?" demanded Babington.

"While it lasts, yes," grimly replied the Constable ; "you may both meet upon Tower-green, if ye survive the horrors of the torture-chamber."

"Farewell, Titchbourne," cried Babington, sadly ; "we meet no more in this world."

"Farewell, Babington," replied Chidiock Titchbourne ; "we but leave a world of care to earn a crown of glory ; we shall suffer for our Queen and our religion. God bless Queen Mary of Scotland."

"Away with the Papistical knaves !" furiously thundered the Constable, in terrible tones ; "away with them, lest I slay them, captives though they be."

Obeying the orders of their chief, the warders hastened the conspirators up the slimy steps, and without a parting word, but with one long look of affectionate farewell, the two conspirators were hurried along separate passages—to meet no more upon this side of the grave.

———

CHAPTER IV.

THE TORTURE-CHAMBER.

SHOWING THE MANNER IN WHICH ANTHONY BABINGTON WAS PUT TO THE TORTURE—HOW HE UNDERWENT THE ORDEALS OF THE SCAVENGER'S DAUGHTER, THE THUMBSCREW, THE RACK, THE LITTLE EASE, THE HEATED SLAB, AND THE RATS' WELL—ALSO OF THE HORRIBLE SENTENCE PASSED UPON HIM.

BENEATH the Bell Tower was the torture-chamber of the ancient fortress—a square-shaped chamber, with a deep, round, arched recess at the right of the entrance.

At the further end of the apartment was a small cell, surmounted with a pointed arch, in the centre of which stood a massive stone pillar.

From this pillar projected a long iron bar, sustaining a coil of rope, terminating by a hook.

On the ground lay an immense pair of pinchers, a curiously-shaped saw, and a brasier.

In one corner lay the rack—a large oaken frame, with ropes and levers in readiness.

At the other was a ponderous wooden machine, like a pair of stocks.

Against the wall hung a broad hoop of iron, and opening in the middle with a knife.

This horrible instrument of torture was termed "The Scavenger's Daughter."

Near it were a pair of iron gauntlets, which could be contracted by screws till they crushed the fingers of the victim.

Opposite the doorway stood another brasier, filled with blazing coals, in which a huge pair of pinchers were thrust.

Reared against the side of the dark recess was a ponderous wheel, as broad in the belly as that of a waggon, and twice the circumference.

This antiquated instrument of torture was placed there to strike terror into the hearts of those who beheld it, for it was rarely used.

Next to it was a heavy bar of iron, employed to break the limbs of the sufferer tied to its spokes.

On the wall hung a small brush, to sprinkle the wretched victims who fainted with excess of agony, with vinegar.

On a table beneath it were placed writing materials and an open volume, in which were taken down the confessions of the sufferers.

At this table sat Sir Henry Bedingfield, the Constable of the Tower, and four other grave-looking personages.

There was no compassion in their faces.

They were inscrutable and inexorable, and scarcely less dreadful to look upon than the hideous implements on the walls.

At this moment the faint chimes of a clock came through the deep embrasure.

It tolled the hour of twelve.

As the last stroke died away, the door opened, and, escorted by Blackblood, the sworn tormentor, Sidley, the gaoler, Ratcliff, the chirurgeon, and Pilate, the executioner, Anthony Babington entered the apartment.

"Anthony Babington," cried the Constable, in stern tones, "are you prepared to confess your crime in thus conspiring against our sovereign lady, the Queen, and against the peace of these realms? Are you prepared to deliver up the names of your associates, and throw yourself upon the clemency of your earthly judges?"

"I am not," was the defiant reply.

"If you persist in this stubborn demeanour," went on the Constable, "the severest measures will be adopted towards you. Your sole chance of avoiding the torture which awaits you is in making a full confession."

"I do not wish to avoid the cruelties that you are disposed to inflict upon me," replied Babington; "your tortures shall wring nothing from me."

"You are not the first who have thought so until they have experienced the horrors of our engines," retorted the Constable, with a meaning gesture.

Babington smiled defiantly, but made no answer.

"You will not speak!" shouted Sir Henry Bedingfield, furiously; "you treat your judges with contempt. But, enough. What, ho, Blackblood! this vile Papist shall be put through all the degrees of torture if he continues thus obstinate. With what shall we commence?"

"With the Scavenger's Daughter and the Little Ease, may it please you, honorable sir," replied the sworn tormentor; "we can then try the gauntlets and the rack; and, if the prisoner then continues refractory, the Rats' Well and the Heated Slab."

"'Fore heaven, a goodly progression!" answered Sir Henry, smiling. "Let us commence without further delay."

Sidley, the gaoler, now took down the broad iron hoop, and, opening the centre hinge, held it in readiness.

The officials looked like evil spirits, but Babington watched their movements with unaltered composure.

Blackblood signified to the Constable that all was ready.

"Your vaunted courage will now be put to the test," remarked Sir Henry, sneering; "let us see if your Papistical bravado will support you."

"What am I to do?" was the calm reply.

"Remove your doublet, and prostrate yourself," said Blackblood.

Babington did as he was desired, and began to recite a prayer to the Virgin.

"Silence, hound, or you shall be gagged!" roared the Constable, with fury.

And now, kneeling upon the prisoner's shoulders, and passing the iron hoop beneath his legs, Blackblood, assisted by the others, who added their weight to his own, succeeded in fastening the hoop with an iron button.

The limbs of the unfortunate victim were now so firmly compressed that he could scarcely breathe.

Blood began to spurt, not only from his mouth and nostrils, but from the extremities of his hands and feet.

For two hours he remained thus.

At length, Ratcliff, the chirurgeon, spoke.

"He must be released," he said, "another five minutes may be fatal."

"He must not die yet," said the Constable, grimly, "take off the hoop."

The Scavenger's Daughter was removed, and now it was that the severest torture took place.

In spite of all his efforts a convulsive effort shook his frame, for the renewal of the impeded circulation and respiration occasioned Babington the most acute agony.

Ratcliff bathed his temples with vinegar, and placing him upon a couch, chafed his aching limbs.

"As you have had a taste of the milder torture," said Sir Henry, "you can now conjecture what the worst may be like. Do you still continue obstinate?"

"I have not changed my mind," was the firm reply, delivered almost in a swooning tone.

"Place him in the thumbscrews!" was the stern order next given.

Without further words, Blackblood and Pilate raised Babington, who was, as yet, too weak to walk, and assisted him into the recess.

Across this was a heavy beam with pulleys and ropes at either extremity.

But what principally attracted the attention of the wretched victim was a couple of iron gauntlets attached to it about a yard apart.

While upon the ground, and immediately beneath the beam in question, were laid three pieces of wood a few inches in thickness, and piled one upon the other.

"What must I do?" inquired Babington, in a hollow voice, but with unchanged resolution.

"Step upon those pieces of wood," said Blackblood, leading him towards them.

Babington obeyed.

Hardly had he set foot upon the pile than the sworn tormentor placed a stool beside him.

Mounting it, Blackblood desired the captive to place one hand within the gauntlet above.

He did so, and then the tormentor turned a screw, which compressed the glove so tightly as to give him excruciating pain.

And now Blackblood placed the stool on the left side, and fastened the hand which was still at liberty in the other gauntlet.

Again the screw turned.

The torture was dreadful, and the fingers appeared crushed.

Still Babington uttered no cry.

At length the Constable spoke,—

"Are we to go on with the question?" he asked. "Beware! for this is but child's play to that which is to follow."

Babington returned no answer.

Then Blackblood took a mallet, and struck one of the pieces of wood from beneath his feet.

The shock was dreadful.

His wrists seemed dislocated.

The pressure on the hands was increased to a tenfold degree.

Babington was now resting upon the points of his feet.

In spite of his fortitude, he knew that the removal of the next piece of wood must occasion him intolerable anguish.

His determination did not, however, desert him.

Once more was he asked to confess.

Still no answer.

And now the second block was knocked away.

The captive was suspended by his hands.

The torture was exquisite.

Nature could bear no more; she gave way;.

and, with a low moan of heartfelt anguish, the wretched captive swooned.

"Unloose him, and take him to the Little Ease," cried Sir Henry Bedingfield, brutally; "he can pass the night there, and he won't find it as comfortable as a feather bed."

A grim smile followed this sally, and the myrmidons of the Constable proceeded to unloose the senseless figure, whose brow was now bathed in the sweats of deadly agony.

Babington was then led out by Pilate and Sidley, and conveyed along a narrow passage till arriving at a low door, in which there was an iron grating.

It was opened.

It then disclosed a cell, four feet in height, a few inches in width, and two feet deep.

Into this narrow receptacle, which was entirely out of proportion to a man of Babington's size, he was with some difficulty thrust, and the door closed upon him.

In this wretched plight, with his head bent upon his breast—for the cell was so built that its wretched inmate could neither sit nor lay at full length within it—Babington, who had recovered himself, prayed long and fervently.

Next morning, Sidley, the gaoler, came, and placed before him a small loaf of black bread and a jug of dirty water.

Scarcely had his scanty meal been ended when Blackblood appeared with a couple of halberdiers, and, desiring him to follow, led the way to the torture chamber.

When Babington crawled in Sir Henry Bedingfield was there.

The Constable demanded in a stern tone—

"Whether ye yet remained obstinate?"

Again did he receive no answer.

"Try him with the rack!"

Babington was seized by Blackblood and Pilate and thrown upon his back. He could make no resistance; even had he possessed the power, it would have been useless.

He determined, however that, even if he expired beneath the torture, he would not let an expression of anguish escape him.

He had need of all his firmness.

The sharpness of the suffering to which his lacerated frame was now subjected was such as few could have withstood.

But not a groan burst from him, though his whole frame seemed rent in twain by the dreadful tension.

"Go on," cried the Constable; "turn the rollers round once more."

"You will wrench his bones from their sockets," replied the chirurgeon; "he will expire if you strain him further."

Again was the question put to him.

Again did Babington return no answer.

And now the Constable ordered that he should suffer the ordeal of the Heated Slab.

This was also placed in the terrible recess.

Within this there was a small furnace in which fuel was placed ready for kindling.

Over the furnace laid a large flag of black marble.

At either end of this were stout leathern straps.

After being again subjected to the interrogatories of the Constable, Babington was stripped of his attire and bound to the flag.

The fire was lighted.

Gradually the stone heated.

The writhing frame of the miserable man ere long showed the extremity of his suffering.

But he did not even utter a groan, and his tormentors at length released the bruised, blistered, and burnt body.

The next phase of torture to which the unfortunate Catholic gentleman was subjected was that of the "Rats' Well."

This was a horrible pit, adjoining the river—called thus from the loathsome animals who infested it.

It was twenty feet wide and twelve deep.

At high tide it was more than two feet deep in water.

Babington was lowered into this horrible chasm.

They warned him of the probable fate which awaited him.

Then they left him in *total darkness.*

Now the pit was free from water.

It was almost dry.

This, however, was not to last long.

The tide was rising.

Frequent splashes convinced the captive that the vermin were at hand.

With a groan he stooped down.

He felt the water.

It was alive with rats.

He felt the walls of the chasm.

The rats were climbing up the roughened surface of the stone.

He knew that they would not long delay their attack.

Prepared for the worst, as he was, he could not

repress a shudder at the prospect of the horrible death with which he was menaced.

Oh, God! he was now surrounded by the rats

They were creeping up the sides of the pit by hundreds, and were preparing to make a general attack upon him.

For the moment he thought that he would let them do their worst.

But the contact of the noxious vermin made him change his resolution.

He drove them off.

Again did they return to the charge, with increased fury.

Self-preservation was the feeling now paramount in his mind.

The fear of being devoured alive inspired his crippled limbs and strained joints with fresh vigor.

He rushed to the other extremity of the pit.

The vermin followed him in myriads.

They sprang upon him.

Their sharp teeth met in his flesh in a thousand places.

In this way the contest continued for some time.

But at length Babington fell, exhausted.

And the whole host darted upon him.

At this instant several gloomy figures were seen at the edge of the pit.

Amongst them Babington distinguished Sir Henry Bedingfield, who instantly offered to release him if he would confess.

"I would rather perish!" was the reply "Ere long I shall be out of the reach of your malice. I care not for my suffering, for I am a martyr in a good cause."

"This must not be," cried the Constable; "drag him forth while I read his condemnation."

A ladder was now let down into the chasm, and Sidley, Blackblood, and Pilate descended.

They were just in time.

Babington had ceased to struggle.

The rats were attacking him.

His words would speedily have been verified but for the timely interposition of the Constable.

They took the bleeding figure out of the pit, and laid it upon the edge of the chasm.

"Listen," cried the Constable; "listen to your sentence. You will be dragged to the spot in Red Lion-court, in Fleet-street, where the "Lion with the opened mouth" once stood—the scene of your bloody and damnable conspiracy—at a horse's tail, and will there be turned off the gallows, and hanged—*but not till you are dead.* While you are yet alive you will be disembowelled; your atrocious

heart will be torn bleeding from your breast; your quarters will be placed on the Gate of Temple-bar, as an abhorrent spectacle in the eyes of men, and a terrible proof of the Queen's just vengeance."

To this Babington returned no answer.

Probably he had not heard a word of it, for, when they examined him, they found that he had fainted.

CHAPTER V.

THE ESCAPE BY THE BELFRY.

SHOWING HOW CHIDIOCK TITCHBOURNE WROTE SOME VERSES UPON THE CASEMENT OF HIS CELL, OF THE MYSTERIOUS MESSAGE THAT HE RECEIVED FROM BALLARD, AND OF THE MANNER IN WHICH HE DESCENDED FROM THE BELFRY, AND MADE HIS ESCAPE FROM THE TOWER OF LONDON.

ROUGHLY cast into the dungeon by the warders, Chidiock Titchbourne sank upon the stone bench within his cell, and burying his face in his hands, gave way to the dismal reflections which assailed him.

A prisoner in the Tower of London, not only himself and Babington, but every one of his fellow conspirators, would no doubt speedily share their fate.

And such a fate.

A fate whose only end was dishonour and death.

The conspiracy had come to nought.

Mary was still a prisoner at Tutbury.

Elizabeth still seated unshaken upon her throne.

How would the unfortunate Queen of Scots bear the terrible blow which had fallen so suddenly?

How terrible would be her anguish of mind at the knowledge that so many brave and noble men would meet a disgraceful death, by their strict adherence to her cause?

Oh! ill-fated House of Stuart—accursed from first to last.

Carefully guarded as was the Queen, by Sir Amias Paulet, the Governor of Tutbury Castle, it was not probable that she would ever hear of the failure of the conspiracy.

These were the questions that Chidiock Titchbourne asked himself, as he sat in the dreary loneliness of his cell, on the night of his arrest.

But when on the morrow, Sidley, the gaoler,

informed him that Anthony Babington was about to be questioned by the sworn tormenter, in the torture chamber, and that he, Titchbourne, had better prepare for the same fate, unless he would confess, not only his share in the conspiracy, but at the same time, reveal the names and titles of all who were associated with the plot; then, indeed, did other ideas fill his mind.

Was there no chance of escape?

No possible means by which he could communicate with the Queen of Scots, and inform her of the failure of the plot, and the probable danger with which she was menaced?

Was it possible to escape from the fortress in which he was imprisoned?

Had anyone ever attempted the almost supernatural feat of forcing their way through the impregnable granite walls, which stood between liberty and himself.

Yes, he recollected one.

An old tradition, relating how, in the year 1234, Griffith, Prince of Wales, while attempting to escape from the White Tower, by a line made of hanging sheets and tablecloths tied together, broke the rope, and, falling from a great height, perished miserably; his head and neck being driven into his breast, between his shoulders.

Would such be his fate?

Even if it was, far better to die in that manner, than by the hands of the common hangman, surrounded by a ribald crowd.

Yes, he would risk it.

He would escape.

But how?

Even while he was considering the means to be employed, a sudden revulsion of feeling came over him, and as he thought how hopeless it would be to make the attempt, he wondered how many noble hearts had slowly fretted and chafed themselves away in that dismal cell.

A host of sad reflections were called up by the perusal of the following lines, which had been cut into the wall, by previous captives.

Taking his lamp, Titchbourne approached the side of the cell, and read them: the first was,—

O Misce Jhon, the pensi ob essere.

The next

Beperus le: sage: et: il: te: aimera. J. S. 1538.

The third

Principium sapientiæ timor Domini, I. II. s. x. r. s. Be friend to one. Be enemye to none—Amos D. 1571, 10th Sept. The most unhappy man in the

would is he that is not patient in adversities. For men are not killed with the adversities that they have, but with the impatience that they suffer. Tout vient apoint, guy scait attendre. Gli supiri ne son testimoni veri del mio interior mal. Æt: 29, Charles Bailly."

"Ah," muttered Chidiock Titchbourne, to himself," these are indeed records of resignation, is it possible that none of these men even had wild visions of escape; have they had no thoughts beyond the misery of their imprisonment; a hope beyond the scaffold;" then, after a moment's reflection, he added, "I will also leave behind me a memento of my imprisonment."

Taking a costly diamond ring off his finger, he approached the strongly barred mullion casement, which admitted light into his room, and wrote the following lines upon the narrow lozenges of glass.

My prime of youth, is but a frost of cares,
  My feast of joy is but a dish of pain
My crop of corn, is but a field of tares,
  And all my goods is but vain hope of grain.
The day is fled, and yet I saw no sun,
  And now I live, and now my life is done!
My spring is past, and yet it hath not sprung,
  The fruit is dead, and yet the leaves are green,
My youth is past, and yet I am but young,
  I saw the world, and yet I was not seen.
My thread is cut, and yet it is not spun,
  And now I live, and now my life is done!
I sought for death, and found it in the womb,
  I look'd for life, and yet it was a shade;
I trod the ground, and knew it was my tomb,
  And now I die, and now I am but made.
The glass is full, and yet my glass is run,
  And now I live, and now my life is done!

Chidiock Titchbourne smiled sadly as he concluded the last line.

"These are, in all likelihood, the last verses that I shall ever compose," he said. "No more sweet rambles to court the muse, in the solitude of the woods and green groves of Upton House and Titchbourne Park."

Further thoughts were, however, out of the question, for Sidley, the gaoler, entered, with the evening meal, consisting of a mess of haricot beans, and a flask of poor sour wine; this, together with a hunch of black bread, composed but a frugal supper.

"This will help you to keep up your strength," grimly remarked Sidley, "for I expect it will be your turn to undergo the examination to-morrow; your leader, Anthony Babington, has been under our hands all this day."

"How has he borne his trials?" eagerly questioned Chidiock, with a thrill of horror passing over him, as in his mind's eye, he conjured up the crushed and mangled form of his friend.

"Hum! bravely—if utter disregard to pain can be called so," replied the gaoler. "For my part, I call it foolhardiness. He has returned no answer to the questions, though we have subjected him to the severest torture. But I expect that the constable will make him speak to-morrow, if he lives till the morning; if he don't confess then, he'll be the only person ever imprisoned in the Tower, whom the sworn tormentor has ever yet failed to make an impression upon."

"I thank God that he has been firm," muttered Chidiock.

"His firmness or obstinacy will save none of you," replied Sidley.

"How?"

"Because the Queen has taken into favour Iscariot, the protestant preacher, who was formerly a monk at the Abbey. It was he who discovered the conspiracy to the Government, and it is he who in future will be attached to the person of Elizabeth. Hope for no mercy, Iscariot has sworn to exterminate from off the face of England all those who adhere to the Catholic religion, be they peer or peasant, and it is at his instigation that the utmost severity will be exercised against all those who were engaged in the Babington conspiracy.

With these words Sidley left the cell, and once more was Chidiock Titchbourne left a prey to his own dismal thoughts.

One idea alone prevaded his mind.

He must escape from the Tower, and make his way to Tutbury Castle.

He had promised Babington that he would do so.

This once done, he would hasten to Spain, and there enrol himself beneath the banner of that country.

At this time the Spanish Armada was fitting out to make a descent upon England, and he would volunteer to take a command in the expedition.

While his mind was thus engrossed with plans for the future, his eyes suddenly fell upon a small roll of parchment which lay near the door of the cell.

A presentiment that the scrap of vellum came from a friend made him leap to his feet, and he gained possession of it.

His suspicions were verified.

Rapidly unrolling it, he read the following cipher:—

"*oo †. oe.—† *k -‡: epoz ep: z:— jpi*v—jc:в zej kj.— :i*v: †— †· ‡cv:o:"—e *— —:kv— —e .*?: !*:†pg —ep —‡: ge*o:c ‡*· !:;p !c†?:в —e o:*?: —‡: Bcec em zejc i:oo ev:p * !e*— !:p:*—‡ clp Bep. !c†Bg —‡†cB,*ci‡ !*oo*cB

Beneath is the translation—

"*All is lost. I am the only one yet uncaptured. You must escape. It is hopeless to attempt to save Babington. The gaoler has been bribed to leave the door of your cell open. A boat beneath London-bridge. Third arch.*

"BALLARD."

Thrusting the precious parchment in his doublet, Chidiock advanced to the door.

The message from Ballard, the Jesuit priest, was correct.

Sidley had earned his bribe.

The door of the cell was open.

Chidiock at once crossed the threshold and found himself at the foot of a winding stone staircase.

This led him into an upper chamber, which was vacant.

The door of this was also open.

Hastily entering the room and shutting the door, which fastened outside with a stout iron bar, he

THE SILENT FRIEND.

then mounted a short flight of wooden steps leading into the loft, where the alarm-bell of the fortress hung.

Carefully walking round the immense bell and gazing with a shudder down to the depth of the interior of the tower, over which swayed the huge clapper, Chidiock Titchbourne gradually approached the aperture which led from the loft on to the leads.

As he did so he cautiously drew back.

For the faint rays of the moon revealed to him that a sentinel was stationed upon the roof, evidently mounting guard over the bell.

The halberdier was carelessly singing to himself.

He had no thought that danger lurked so near him.

Even had his suspicions been aroused, any effort upon his part would have been fruitless.

With a sudden bound, more like the spring of a tiger than a human being, Chidiock Titchbourne sprang upon the soldier, who was leaning upon his partizan, and ere he could utter an exclamation, a blow from his own weapon had stretched him senseless upon the leads.

And now not an instant was to be lost.

Titchbourne's plan of action was rapidly formed.

Drawing the soldier's sword from its sheath, he cut one of the huge coils of rope used to ring the alarm bell.

Drawing this up from the depths below, he then quickly fastened it to one of the stout supporters of the belfry.

Then he flung the coil over the battlements, and prepared to descend by it.

Endowed with great strength and activity, the result of his country training, Chidiock Titchbourne rapidly descended the rope.

The roughened surface of the old walls, and other irregularities in the structure, against which he placed his feet, were of material aid to him.

So that Chidiock reached the ground in safety.

His descent had not been noticed on account of the darkness, though, when his foot touched the earth he found a small knot of halberdiers conversing scarce a dozen paces away.

Cautiously creeping past them, he hastened towards the drawbridge.

Here he encounted the priest, Iscariot, who immediately recognised him, and, with a shout of vengeance, tried to intercept him.

But without bandying words with the renegade, Chidiock hurled him violently back and dashed onwards.

In a voice of thunder Iscariot gave the alarm.

His cries were immediatly answered by a party of halberdiers, who rushed out of the adjoining guard-room.

They were all armed with pikes, arquebuses, and calivers.

Seizing a torch from a warder who stood near him, Iscariot hastened after the fugitive with the howl of a disappointed fiend.

By this time the flight of Chidiock from his cell had been discovered.

And now the alarm bell began to ring.

Word was passed to the sentinel right round the line of the fortifications that a prisoner had escaped.

All was in commotion in an instant.

Torches gleamed along the whole line of ramparts, and cast a lurid glare upon the dark waters of the moat.

Everywhere, voices rose in hoarse shouts.

Soldiers and warders hastened to each point where there was a chance of the fugitive breaking forth.

Another shout was raised, for, by the light of the torches, Chidiock Titchbourne could be seen swimming across the moat.

Shots were fired at the fugitive from the summit of the Byward Tower.

But they merely speckled the water without doing any damage.

Scrambling out of the moat upon the wharf, Chidiock Titchbourne was speedily lost in the darkness.

The drawbridge was lowered, and a hot pursuit commenced, but without avail.

Chidiock Titchbourne had ESCAPED FROM THE TOWER.

CHAPTER VI

TUTBURY CASTLE.

SHOWING HOW JOHN BALLARD AND CHIDIOCK TITCHBOURNE JOURNEYED TO TUTBURY—HOW THEY MET GIFFORD, THE PRIEST, AND MADE THEIR ENTRANCE INTO THE CASTLE.

SNOW everywhere !

Snow lading the boughs of ancient trees.

Snow, hiding from mortal sight the rank grass and weeds of a desolate Staffordshire moor.

Snow clinging round the feet of weary pedestrians, and clogging the hoofs of jaded steeds.

A dull November fog hovering over the whole prospect, imparting to the glorious landscape a gloomy, death-like aspect.

A bitter north-east wind hustling over the dreary waste.

The icy breath, enveloping all who encountered it in an impassable but frozen garment.

Icicles, long, huge icicles, depending from the sloping roofs of the thatched cottages which studded the scene.

Across the bleak, comfortless moor were three gibbets, laden with the ghastly skeletons of some highwaymen, whose sad remains hung in chains.

The whole landscape blank, save with the exception of a couple of horsemen, who were travelling rapidly, side by side.

Both were evidently well mounted.

The elder bestrode a grey mare of the Flanders breed.

The younger, a grey horse, whose splendid action bespoke an Arabian sire.

As our readers will surmise, the eldest of the riders was the Jesuit, John Ballard—or rather, Captain Fortescue—for it was under this *alias* that he was better known—

While his companion was no other than our hero, Chidiock Titchbourne.

"Mother of Grace!" ejaculated the latter; "already am I tired almost unto the death. Have we long to journey yet, father?"

"But another fifteen miles, my son," replied the priest, in a weary tone; "we have scarce drawn rein since last night. I would fain rest myself; but we have a great stake yet to play for, and, alas! I fear me much that we are the only two who have thus escaped to work for our cause."

"We will not lose heart, dear father," cried Chidiock; "we shall yet strike a desperate blow for our Queen and country."

"I have but little hope of success," answered Ballard, mournfully; "nought but misfortune has ever been the fate of those who have borne the name of Stuart, and I fear me that such will ever be their portion."

"Our Lady of Nazarene aid us!" prayed Chidiock; "there may be yet a chance, good father, and neither neglect or delay upon our part must place obstacles in the path which we have sworn to pursue."

"You are right, my son, so let us hasten onwards," replied Ballard; "in a short time the turrets of Tutbury Castle will be within view, and there, with the assistance of Gifford, we shall be able to seek shelter, and gain admittance to the presence of Mary, Queen of Scots."

"I trust that we shall have no difficulty in so doing," said Chidiock, uneasily.

"Have no fear; the seminary priest, Gifford, knows of our coming, and all will be arranged," replied Ballard.

Without another word the two rapidly spurred on, and, as Ballard had intimated, the turrets of Tutbury speedily appeared in sight.

It may be interesting to the reader to give a description of the Castle in which the unfortunate Queen of Scots was confined.

Since the sun had sunk a thick mist had overspread the landscape.

Above this mist, and high upon the wood-clad hill upon whose summit they were mounted, rose the turrets and towers of Tutbury Castle.

At the foot of the hill rolled the turbid waters of the river, the waves of which were lashed into a white foam by the bitter wind, as it rushed along its course.

The edifice at whose foot it rolled had been deserted for so great a length of time that its towers were covered with creeping ivy, deadly nightshade, nettles, and many other herbal parasites.

Three sides of the prison of the wretched Queen were surrounded by a deep fosse, and a high, embattled wall.

On the north side was the drawbridge, and a huge portcullis.

This latter was the principal entrance to the Castle.

The whole building was, however, greatly dilapidated, and was rapidly sinking to decay.

The northern tower had a huge cleft from the summit to the basement, and this opening was garlanded with ivy and crusted with moss.

The splashing of the black waters of the moat, the measured tramp of the sentinels, and the muffled sound of their horses' hoofs were the only signs of life that struck upon the ears of the travellers as they approached the building.

Halting beneath the shadow of a dark copse, situated upon the edge of the moat, Ballard and Chidiock hastened to confer together.

"It is here," muttered Ballard, in a low tone, "that Gifford is to meet us."

Then raising his hand with a warning gesture, the Jesuit went on—

"Hark! I am not deceived. He is here."

As he spoke a low and cautious whistle fell upon their ears.

At the same moment a dark figure emerged

from beneath the gloom of the trees, and advanced towards them.

"Peace be with you, Father Ballard, and also with thee, my son."

"May thou also share it, Father Gifford," replied Ballard. "But, come, haste, and tell us of the news."

"All is well," was the reply; "the Queen does not yet know of the failure of the conspiracy in London. She has been too closely guarded by Sir Amias Paulet; even I have not been able to obtain admittance to her presence."

"Our journey is then for nought," cried Titchbourne, sorrowfully.

"Not so," rejoined Gifford; "I have made all arrangements for the interview. Ere the night has passed you shall both be with Queen Mary."

"Ah! now you raise our hopes indeed," said Ballard, cheerfully. "Methought that another disappointment was about to be added to those which have already crushed our souls."

"Art thou ready to accompany me now?" was the next question that Gifford asked, with a curious change in his voice, which, however, fell unheeded upon the ears of his companions.

"Ready, aye, and right willing, too," replied Titchbourne; "I had almost feared, like our good Father Ballard here, that thy tidings were of a more dismal nature."

"Be of good cheer," replied Gifford, with a sinister smile, which was, however, hidden in the darkness. "Be of good cheer, for let me assure you that our great cause is not lost yet, even after the failure of the club in London, for we have yet many stout hearts in the North, and numberless brawny arms, only waiting for the moment when they shall be called upon to aid us in thrusting the queenly prisoner of Tutbury upon the throne of England."

"Bravely and right worthily spoken, good Father," cried Titchbourne; "but let us on; we have little time for thought, still less for action. Our word must now be 'Action, and the foremost to the front.'"

Gifford now commenced to lead the way to a shed which stood some three hundred yards distant.

Carefully guiding their horses over the undulating surface of the frozen ground, Ballard and Titchbourne followed their guide.

"You can stable your steeds within these walls," remarked Gifford; "they will here be secured

from observation; and within this place lays the thoroughfare which will convey us, without notice, within the precincts of the Castle."

"You mean——" began Ballard, whose plotting brain immediately conceived the contrivance hinted at—

"I mean that there is a secret entrance here which leads beneath the fosse," interrupted Gifford.

"How came you to learn of it?" demanded Ballard, an undefinable suspicion, which he could not analyse, creeping over him.

"From Sir Amias Paulet, who believes that I am devoted to his interests," replied Gifford. Then he added, defiantly, "Why do you ask in that tone? Had it not been for my duplicity and seeming compliance with the views of Elizabeth and those who surround her, I had never have held the position I now occupy, or have been able to have succoured our beloved mistress."

"Pardon my warmth," said Ballard; "but, surrounded, as we are, by enemies on all sides, a feeling of suspicion comes over us, even when in the company of those whom we know are true to the cause."

"It would be as well, perhaps," rejoined Gifford, in an offended and somewhat threatening tone, "if you were not so suspicious, but it's as well, perhaps," he continued, menacingly; "it is as well to be upon your guard, for in this world we cannot always distinguish our friends from our enemies."

"Come, enough of this," broke in Chidiock; "this wrangling is unseemly, good Fathers. I prithee let us hasten onwards."

By mutual concession neither of the priests spoke again, and both Ballard and Chidiock Titchbourne dismounted, and led their horses into the shed, where they found an abundance of fodder."

Enjoining upon his companions the strictest silence, Gifford commenced to remove with his feet a quantity of straw which encumbered a corner of the shed, and disclosed to view a trapdoor, which was raised by a huge iron ring."

Raising this, and motioning Ballard and Titchbourne to follow him, Gifford cautiously descended the slimy steps which led downwards, and the trio disappeared in the subterranean passage, while Gifford lowered the trap-door, which he carefully fastened.

As he did so, a malicious smile spread over his countenance.

CHAPTER VII.

MARY, QUEEN OF SCOTS.

SHOWING HOW TITCHBOURNE AND BALLARD WERE INTRODUCED INTO THE PRESENCE OF THE IMPRISONED QUEEN—OF THE CONVERSATION THAT ENSUES—HOW THE DESIGNS OF GIFFORD, THE SEMINARY PRIEST, BECAME UNVEILED—AND OF THE TERRIBLE TRAP INTO WHICH THE CONSPIRATORS FELL.

ILL-FATED Mary, Queen of Scotland, aye, and by right, Queen of England, too, reclined upon a couch in her prison home.

By the tacit behaviour of heartless Elizabeth, by the harshness of Walsingham and other evil councillors who sought her favor, Mary Stuart had been deprived not only of every comfort, but even of absolute necessaries.

Poor, helpless Queen—misjudged and vilified even by modern historians—she lay there, a prey to the agonising sensations of suspense.

Daily, nay, hourly, had she expected tidings from Anthony Babington respecting the conspiracy, which, if successful, was to place her upon the throne—which, if a failure, would end her imprisonment with an ignominious death.

It was either the Throne or the Scaffold.

Mary Stuart knew this, and, with a placid resignation, almost angelic in its intensity, she was prepared to meet the fate that destiny had in store for her.

The Queen had already been apprised, and was awaiting the arrival of Gifford with the two conspirators who had so daringly ventured into her presence.

Near the Queen lay a lute upon which she had been playing a few plaintive bars of a sweet old Scottish melody.

But now the instrument had fallen from her hand, and her eyes were fixed with painful intensity upon the worm-eaten tapestry, masking a secret door through which Gifford visited her.

This entrance was unknown to anyone save Gifford, who professed to have been told of the secret passage by one of the retainers, whom he had bribed.

The night wind whistled through the crevices of the ruined walls, and swayed the tapestry to and fro, distorting the huge faces woven upon it, and giving them a terribly life-like appearance.

The meagre lamp which lit the apartment only seemed to render the darkness still more palpable, and the further end of the room was enveloped in obscurity.

The handsome faces of the murdered Rizzio and Darnley seemed to gaze upon her from the darkest portion of the apartment, while, above all the phantoms of the past which were flitting around, there seemed to peer forth the malevolent countenance of her vindictive cousin—Elizabeth, Queen of England.

The dismal reverie into which the unfortunate lady had fallen was, however, speedily dispelled, for the tapestry was thrust aside, and Jessie Campbell—the only attendant that was allowed about her person—entered.

"Gracious mistress!" cried the pretty Scotch girl, "my watch hath been rewarded; those whom thou hast expected crave an audience of your majesty."

"Bid them enter, my child," replied the Queen.

Jessie tripped lightly across the dismal chamber, and, holding the tapestry aside, gave admittance to Gifford, Ballard and Chidiock Titchbourne.

Catching a view of the Queen, Chidiock hastened forward and prostrated himself at her feet.

"Rise, good sir, I prithee," cried Mary, extending her hand towards her devoted follower. "Rise; but little royalty surrounds me now; I would fain be looked upon by my friends no longer as a queen, but as an unfortunate and much misjudged lady.

"Not so, my daughter," cried Ballard, raising one hand towards heaven; "not so, however clouded and overcast our horizon may appear for the time, the day must come when not only in England, but over the whole surface of the civilized globe, the most holy catholic religion shall reign paramount.

"I fervently trust that such will be the case," sighed Mary, with passionate ardour.

Then, noticing their disordered apparel; and averted glances, she went on.

"What news have you brought me, gentlemen? Ha! fresh tidings of evil; I can see in your manner, do not hesitate—speak, I conjure you."

And Mary rose from her couch, and advanced towards them.

Ballard again spoke.

"Bear well and bravely against this fresh affliction, my daughter. The conspiracy has failed—"

"Then all is lost!"

And the Queen bitterly wrung her hands.

"Not so! gracious lady," broke in Chidiock Titchbourne. "Not so, we will yet strike another blow."

"No, no," murmured Mary. "It is useless; the hand of heaven is against the House of Stuart."

"Pause, daughter, ere you revile your Maker," cried Ballard, solemnly. "Titchbourne is right; another blow must, and shall be struck; another effort made."

"Be it so then, Father," rejoined the Queen, recovering a portion of her energy of purpose. "Be it so—but one question, Anthony Babington, the brave and noble Babington, why does he not accompany you?"

"Alas! gracious mistress," said Titchbourne, with emotion. "We shall never behold him more."

"Ha! what mean you, sir?"

"That Babington is confined in the Tower of London, daughter," said Ballard. "That, for the sake of his religion and his queen, he has endured every torture that the most devilish ingenuity could devise, and yet hath he remained steadfast and firm to those with whom he was leagued."

Mary sank back upon her couch, overpowered by the intelligence.

"One by one my brave followers suffer and die," she murmured, while tears of anguish rapidly coursed down her fair face.

"Oh! God of mercies, this must not be, father; no further attempt must be made to reinstate me upon the throne, no more brave hearts must be sacrificed for my sake."

Ballard did not answer his royal mistress, and motioned Titchbourne not to speak.

Then after a few moment's silence, he related to the Queen the discovery of the conspiracy, the arrest of Babington and Titchbourne, and the escape of the latter from the Tower.

Hardly had Ballard concluded his recital, and ere the Queen had sufficiently regained her self-possession to reply, than Jessie Campbell again entered the apartment, this time by the ordinary door.

Her whole appearance was suggestive of the greatest terror.

The wildness of her looks alarmed all present, with the exception of Gifford, over whose features a smile of sinister moment flitted, and then disappeared.

"What means this unseemly haste, child?" demanded Ballard."

"Oh! Father of Goodness, what new tribulation awaits us?" gasped the Queen, the ashy pallor of her countenance deepening as a spasm smote her heart with the knowledge of approaching danger.

"They are upon us—they are upon us," incoherently cried the handmaiden.

"Upon us! whom?" demanded Titchbourne, with his hand upon the hilt of his rapier.

"Sir Amias Paulet, with half the soldiers of the garrison at his back," replied the frightened girl, in trembling accents.

"Betrayed," cried Gifford, with well-feigned fright, sinking, as he spoke, into a corner of the apartment.

"Betrayed!" muttered Ballard and Titchbourne together, at the same time drawing their swords, while a fierce determination to sell their lives as dearly as possible took possession of both.

"Is there no means of escape," said Mary. "You must not, nay, shall not be slain before mine eyes, as was the unfortunate Rizzio."

"Yes, the secret entrance behind the arras," cried Jessie.

With one accord, Ballard and Titchbourne rushed towards it.

As they did so, a smile of evil meaning overspread the features of Gifford.

"Too late, too late!" he muttered between his clenched teeth.

With a cry of disappointment, Ballard found that the masked entrance was closed.

It resisted all his efforts to open it.

Gifford was appealed to.

"We have no hope of escape," replied the traitor priest. "The door closes with a spring lock, once shut, it can but be opened from without."

"Caught, like rats in a trap," cried Titchbourne; "but we'll fight hard ere they capture us—better to die thus than upon the scaffold."

"Rightly spoken, my son, we will fight to the last. What, ho! Father Gifford, hast thou no weapon to raise in defence of the great cause for which we fight?"

"I will neither fight, nor aid you to do so," was the reply, which fell like a thunder clap upon the ears of his astounded listeners. "We have no chance of escape; let us surrender and trust to the clemency of Elizabeth."

"Never! thou traitorous hound, to counsel honest Englishmen thus," shouted Titchbourne. "Henceforth I shall count thee as a rank and pestilent enemy to our queen and religion, ordained priest though thou art."

As our hero concluded his speech, the tramp of

armed men could be distinctly heard approaching the room."

"Your cause is lost, I tell you, impetuous hot-headed fool," cried Gifford, roused to fury by the words of Titchbourne. "Lost! utterly lost; Walsingham and Burleigh, Elizabeth's wary counsellors, are cognizant of the correspondence that has been sent to yonder puny puppet queen," and he pointed jeeringly at Mary as he spoke, "even the likenesses of those connected with the conspiracy which was drawn by Anthony Babington, has passed before Elizabeth's government, and every man connected with the conspiracy is known."

"Ha! and who has been the traitor?" furiously demanded Ballard.

"I HAVE!" laughed Gifford; "I the poor jesuit priest from the seminary at Rheims."

"'Fore heaven and our Lady," cried Mary, "this traitorous conduct passeth all endurance."

"He shall not live to repent his undoing."

And Titchbourne thrust furiously at the traitor with his sword.

But almost at the same instant, a *posse* of armed men entered the room and threw themselves upon Ballard and Titchbourne.

Gifford was wrenched from their grasp.

With a loud scream of anguish, Mary, Queen of Scots swooned away in the arms of Jessie Campbell, while the two conspirators were hastily bound and hurried from the apartment.

CHAPTER VIII.

IN CAPTIVITY.

HOW THE CONSPIRATORS WERE CONVEYED TO LONDON BY AN ARMED ESCORT. — OF THE MANNER IN WHICH THEY HALTED FOR THE NIGHT, AND OF THE STRANGE MANNER IN WHICH THEY ESCAPED FROM THE HANDS OF THEIR CAPTORS.

Now Ballard and Chidiock Titchbourne were heavily manacled and thrust in a strong room, only to be taken to London on the following day, there to expiate their treason upon the scaffold.

After passing a wretched night upon the damp straw which was strewed upon the floor of their cell, and, unable to interchange ideas with each other, for they had both been gagged as well as bound, the two prisoners were aroused by the entrance of Sir Amias Paulet with half a dozen soldiers.

The latter had come to convey them back to the Tower.

"Remove their gags," cried Sir Amias, in stern tones.

This order was obeyed.

"Now, prisoners," went on the Knight, harshly, "these men will escort you to the scene of your treasonable plots, you will find that your bold attempt to seek an audience of Mary Stuart will result in her downfall, and you can leave here with the consciousness that you have irremediably injured the woman whom you had hoped to place upon the throne of these realms."

"Alas!" muttered Ballard, "I fear that through the treachery of Gifford, our cause is for ever ruined."

"There is hope whilst there is life," rejoined Titchbourne, whose ear the words alone reached.

"Ha! what mean you?" cautiously asked the Priest.

"That the distance from here to London is long," replied Chidiock, in the same low tone, "and there may be a chance of escape."

"I fear not, my son."

"Hope that there may be, father."

"The gags shall again be thrust into your mouths," cried Sir Amias in a voice of thunder, "if you dare but speak again. "Away with them," he continued, turning to the soldiers, "and mind that you will answer for their safe delivery with your lives."

Thus speaking, the governor of Tutbury Castle turned upon his heel and left the cell.

Shortly afterwards, the prisoners, who had no chance of exchanging another sentence, were removed into the court-yard, where a waggon was in waiting.

They were thrust into this, and while one of the soldiers took his seat upon the box, the others mounted their chargers, and the cavalcade slowly passed through the great iron gates of the castle, which had been opened to give them egress.

They journeyed the whole of that day, halting but once upon the road, where the two conspirators partook of some meagre refreshment.

As the shades of evening began to gather, and darkness descended upon the snow-clad landscape, they stopped before a small cottage upon the high road and aroused its solitary inmate.

An old woman answered their boisterous demands for admittance, and when the soldiers asked for shelter and refreshment, she readily placed before them what simple viands she possessed.

The prisoners noticed her readiness with no

little surprise for during the turbulent times of which we are writing, the soldiers were held in but little favour by the peasantry, and when the old woman had gleaned from the troopers what and whom their prisoners were, it was with feelings of gratitude that the conspirators saw that, unperceived by their escort, she bestowed many compassionate glances upon them.

Once or twice she approached them with the intention of proffering some little attention to alleviate the wretched condition they were in, but each attempt was rudely repulsed by the halberdier who had charge of them.

Having satiated themselves with the provisions that were in the house, and grumbling at the insufficiency of the supply, the soldiers prepared to snatch a few hour's rest upon the floor of the hovel.

Five of them remained on guard below, while Ballard and Titchbourne, in charge of the sixth, was conveyed to an upper chamber.

"Be of good cheer, father," whispered Chidiock, "I have a presentiment that our deliverance is at hand."

"Indulge in no false hopes, my son ; we have, I fear, run the length of the tether."

The two conspirators had no time for another word, for they at this moment entered the room allotted to them, and threw themselves upon a rude mattress in a corner of the apartment, while their vigilant guard took up a position near the door.

Both Ballard and Titchbourne fell into an uneasy, fitful slumber, overcome with utter weariness.

Restless, wretched, with minds ill at ease, their sleep was light and broken.

A few hours thus passed away, and, as the grey morning light stole through the casement, Chidiock was aroused by a hand being placed upon his arm.

Thoroughly awoke, he looked upwards, and beheld the old woman bending over him.

Her finger was placed upon her lips, and her whole expression enjoined the strictest silence.

Chidiock understood her gesture.

He felt that his presentiment was right.

He *knew* that the hour of deliverance had come.

But, how ?

In what manner ?

This was speedily explained.

Looking round, he saw the sentinel extended upon the floor, lifeless.

The hands of the trooper were clenched, as if in dire agony.

A frightful expression of pain contracted his features.

The clammy dews of death had gathered on his brow.

Bringing her lips close to the ear of Titchbourne, the old woman muttered, impressively—

"Hush ! for your lives' sake, hush !"

"What is this ?" vacantly demanded Chidiock, pointing to the corpse.

"*Poison !*"

"Poison !" muttered Titchbourne.

"Aye, poison," replied the woman, fiercely—his death and your deliverance. Arouse your companion ; you have no time to lose."

Ballard was speedily awakened and made acquainted with the change that had taken place.

"The troopers who remained below have left the house to prepare their horses ere they renew their march," went on the woman, rapidly. "This wretch was poisoned by a flask of wine, impregnated with a deadly powder, that I had given him to while away his lonely watch. But, come, hasten out of this dwelling ere they return, or you are indeed lost."

"Why have you taken this interest in us ?" demanded Ballard, suspiciously.

"Because I and my sons are strict adherents to the cause of Mary Stuart," replied the woman. "Even now my two eldest boys have left me to join the armed force which Captain Abington is raising."

"Abington !" cried Titchbourne ; "thank God, he has escaped. Are we near his mansion, good mother ?"

"Within five miles from hence, and upon the London road, you will come in sight of Maismore Grange. Once there, you will be in comparative safety. But lose no more time ; hasten away, or it will be too late."

The captives did not require to be admonished again.

Rising to their feet, they followed the woman into the room below, which they found empty, as she had told them.

Hardly had they entered the place than a sudden scream from their companion caused them to look up.

Their consternation may be imagined when they saw a stalwart trooper advancing towards the house.

With a shout of surprise, he advanced towards

them, and, drawing a brace of petronels, commanded them to surrender.

The conspirators were too much taken by surprise, and too enfeebled, to offer resistance.

Calling upon the old woman to fetch a rope to bind them, the trooper unloosed his girdle, and proceeded to fasten Ballard's arms behind his back.

In doing this he was compelled to lay down his petronels.

He had scarcely done this when the woman snatched them up, and gave them to Chidiock Titchbourne, who presented them at the soldier's head.

It was now the turn of the conspirators to triumph.

In another instant Ballard was released by the old woman.

The two then threw themselves upon the trooper and forced him to the ground.

They then dragged him into the back room and stripped him of his habiliments.

These Ballard put on instead of his own.

They then bound the soldier hand and foot, and, having done so, returned to the old woman.

At the request of our hero, she furnished him with a suit of clothes belonging to one of her sons, and bade them hasten away.

Nothing loth, they offered the woman a handsome reward, which she refused to take; the two conspirators then left the humble dwelling, and pursued their way across the fields in the direction of Maismore Grange.

———

CHAPTER IX.

ROYALISTS AND REBELS.

OF THE MANNER IN WHICH THE CONSPIRATORS MET AT MAISMORE GRANGE—OF THE RESOLUTIONS THEY FORMED—HOW THE EXPEDITION SET OUT, AND THE CASTLE OF STAFFORD TAKEN.

THE two conspirators hastened onwards.

With unabated impetuosity, they soon cleared four miles of their journey, and could discern the towers of Maismore Grange rising above the fog, when they overtook a solitary horseman, who proved to be Charles Tilner, and as they neared the mansion they came up with Robert Gage and Henry Donne.

All were mounted, save Ballard and Chidiock Titchbourne.

The two latter, after exchanging greetings with their fellow-conspirators, who had thus far succeeded in escaping safely from London, clung on to the saddles of Gage and Donne, and, thus assisted, speedily arrived at the residence of Abington.

They found the house full of guests, principally composed of those who were engaged in the Babington Plot, and their adherents.

They were just sitting down to supper when Ballard rushed into the room, covered, like those who accompanied him, with dirt and mud.

Their haggard looks and dejected appearance plainly showed those who were not already aware of it, that, for the time, the project had failed.

"All is lost!" cried the Priest; "our scheme has been discovered; Babington is a prisoner; and, ere long, we shall all be led to the scaffold!"

"I will never be led thither with life?" cried Bernard Douglas, a Scottish gentleman who had lately joined the conspiracy.

"Nor I," said John Travers, in a determined tone. "Though the great design has failed, we have yet swords to draw, and, thank our Lady, arms to wield them."

"No, no!" cried Titchbourne; "we will not yield without a blow."

And as the valiant young Englishman spoke, he poured out a bumper of wine and swallowed it at a draught.

"You are right, my son, replied Ballard; "we will sell our lives dearly. Our blood may flow, but it shall flow to the everlasting glory of the Church."

"If we all adhere to this resolution," said Bernard Douglas, "we may yet retrieve our loss. I have six hundred royal Scottish men, who will stand by me to the death; and if all will follow my example, we will raise such a rebellion in England as shall never be checked save by the acknowledgment of our rights and the dethronement of the usurper, Elizabeth."

"We will all stand by you," cried all those assembled.

"Swear it!" shouted Ballard, raising a glass to his lips. "Swear it," he repeated, in solemn tones. "Swear by the holy Church!"

"We do; we will," was the unanimous cry.

And every glass was raised.

"Wearied as we are, we must at once assemble together those who are ready to join our standard," cried Thomas Salisbury.

"Our standard once displayed, cried Titchbourne, enthusiastically, "every Catholic in Staffordshire, in Cheshire, Lancashire, and Wales will flock round it. Even with those we have already around us, we can offer such a stand as will enable us to make conditions with our opponents, aye, or even engage with them, with a prospect of success."

"To arms, then! To arms!" cried the conspirators, emptying their flasks of wine, and flinging the vessels down.

"To arms! To arms!"

The martial cry roused all to the highest point of enthusiasm.

Wild shouts filled the air.

They forgot the terrible odds that were likely to be arrayed against them.

They were moved by one impulse, one motive—the downfall of Elizabeth and the rising of Mary Stuart.

The conspirators now repaired to the court yard.

Here they called over the muster roll of their men, to see that none were missing.

They next carefully examined their arms and ammunition,

Finding all in order, they sprang to their steeds, and placing themselves at the head of the band, rode towards Stafford.

Kept marching the whole night, it was day-break ere the party reached the outskirts of the town.

Having ridden nearly thirty miles over heavy and miry roads, for a huge quantity of rain had fallen during the night, they stood in need of some refreshment.

They accordingly made a raid upon the first farm yard which they espied.

The cow-houses and sheepfolds were speedily emptied of their inmates, whose places were taken by the horses of the conspirators.

The latter set before their jaded steeds whatever provender they could lay their hands upon.

Those again who could find no better accommodation, fed their horses in the yard, which was literally strewn with great trusses of hay and heaps of corn.

The whole scene would have made a curious picture.

The conspirators, gentlemen and commoners, attired in every possible costume.

Here a party driving away towards the fields the bleating sheep and lowering cattle.

Another robbing a hen roost, and coolly wringing the necks of its cackling inmates.

A third preparing to put an end to the existence of a fine porker, who struggled and fought, and squealed loudly for dear life, in the arms of half a dozen of the amateur butcher's comrades.

A fourth, fifth, and sixth, under the direction of Chidiock Titchbourne, harnessing the stoutest horses possessed by the wretched farmer, to the strongest carts upon the farm, with the intention of converting them into baggage waggons.

The horses fed, the next care of the conspirators was to obtain something for themselves.

They ordered the farmer, who was terrified out of his senses, to open his doors.

Not daring to refuse, the man complied with the order.

The conspirators entered the dwelling, and speedily commenced to light huge fires in the principal rooms.

There was fortunately a good store of provisions in the larder.

These were consumed with almost magical rapidity.

A huge cask of strong ale, and another of perry were likewise broached, and a small keg of *Aqua Vitæ* being discovered, it was disposed of in the same way.

Beyond this, there was little mischief done by the principal conspirators, amongst whom Titchbourne and Ballard were the most conspicuous, who spread themselves amongst the band, and checked any disposition to plunder.

A couple of hours had passed away for rest and refreshment, when Captain Abington gave the word to those under his command to prepare to set forth.

In a few moments all were in the saddle.

The farmer's carts were laden with arms and ammunition, and a few sacks of corn.

The line was formed.

The march again commenced.

The morning was dark and misty.

All looked dull and dispiriting.

The chief of the company were, however, full of confidence.

The meal had refreshed and exhilarated both themselves and their men.

The whole band were in the highest possible spirits.

All longed for an opportunity to distinguish themselves.

They had now arrived within half a mile of the old castle of Stafford.

A short consultation was held by the rebel leaders, upon the expediency of attacking the castle.

Keeping possession of it with a part of their force.

And, above all, to carry off the horses with which they had learnt that its stables were well filled.

The consultation was brief.

The boldness of the idea filled all with admiration for Chidiock Titchbourne, who had proposed it.

They at once decided upon making the attempt.

Assembling their followers around them, they communicated the resolution at which they had arrived.

It was received with loud acclamations.

Captain Abington and Chidiock Titchbourne then placed themselves at the head of the band.

Titchbourne rushed forward to an embattled gate, which commanded the approach to the castle.

At this he commenced furiously knocking.

A wicket was opened by an old porter.

The aged servitor started back in terror upon beholding the intruders.

He endeavoured to close the wicket.

Titchbourne saw the intention.

With the quickness of thought, he leaped from his steed.

In another instant, the feeble opposition of the old man was dashed aside, and the gate unbarred.

Instantly mounting, he galloped along a broad and winding path cut so deeply into the rock that the structure which they were approaching was completely hidden from view.

At the end of this was the castle moat, crossed by a drawbridge.

This was down.

The approach of so many horsemen, however, aroused some of the retainers, who rushed forth.

They were too late to raise it.

Threatening these servitors with instant death if they offered the least resistance, Abington, Titchbourne, and Ballard passed through the great entrance, guarded by a portcullis.

Riding into the court, they drew up their band around them.

Terrified and alarmed, the whole of the inmates of the castle now collected upon the ramparts.

They were armed with calivers and partisans.

Though their force was utterly disproportioned to that of the conspirators, still they seemed disposed to give them battle.

Paying no heed to them, the principal conspirators proceeded to the stables.

Here they found forty horses.

They were speedily exchanged for the most jaded of the band.

Titchbourne and Ballard, with some half dozen of their followers, now proceed to enter the castle to search for arms.

They suddenly paused.

The alarm bell had began to ring.

At the same moment, a culverin was discharged from the summit of the tower.

Thomas Salisbury hastened to the belfry, where he speedily silenced the bell.

Leaving a man in charge, he returned to the conspirators with information of a startling nature.

The inhabitants of Stafford were assembling.

Drums were being beaten at the gates; an attack might be momentarily expected.

No time was to be lost.

It would not be prudent to risk an engagement at that juncture.

This feeling was shared by the whole of the conspirators.

They gave up the idea of ransacking the castle, and at once ordered their men to be mounted.

This was not effected without delay.

Bell kept ringing.

Drums beating.

An occasional shot fired.

" By Heaven," cried Chidiock, " we shall have the whole country upon us."

"The more the merrier," replied old Captain Abington, with a careless laugh. " But come, let us see what fate has in store for us."

The troops were now assembled.

They crossed the draw-bridge, and again sped along the rocky path.

Before the outer gate was a large body of men.

Some mounted.

Some on foot.

Many of them, however, alarmed at the formidable appearance of the conspirators retreated, and allowed them a free passage.

A little further on they found the road occupied by a strong well-armed body of men.

The Sheriff of Stafford was at their head.

These men showed no disposition to give way.

The conspirators made preparations to force a passage.

At this moment a trumpet sounded.

The Sheriff rode towards them.

In the Queen's name he commanded them to yield themselves prisoners.

"We do not acknowledge the supremacy of Elizabeth," sternly rejoined Titchbourne. "We fight for the restoration of the holy catholic religion, which we profess."

"Yield! Chidiock Titchbourne," cried the Sheriff; then turning towards the conspirators, he cried, "Englishmen, throw down your arms and deliver up your leaders; in the Queen's name I offer a free pardon to you—and a hundred pounds who will bring me the head of either John Ballard or Chidiock Titchbourne."

The answer that the Sheriff received was from Charles Tilney, who levelled a petronel and shot him dead.

The fall of the Sheriff was a signal for a general engagement.

The Royalist party assailed the conspirators with the greatest fury.

Cheering on their men, Titchbourne and Abington fought through their foes, and slowly made their way back to the bridge.

Here they made a desperate rally.

The day had turned, fortune was now with the conspirators.

Once within the castle again they could defy all attacks from without.

Chidiock and his men had almost made good their retreat, when to his horror and dismay, Titchbourne saw that John Ballard was a prisoner in the hands of the Royalists.

Regardless of all consequences, Chidiock shouted to those near him to follow him.

So desperate and headlong was the charge that he made, that in a few minutes he was beside Ballard, and had succeeded in liberating him.

Now he in his turn became separated from his companions.

On all sides was he hotly pressed.

His destruction seemed inevitable.

The barrels of his petronels were empty.

His sword was shivered close to the hilt.

Defenceless as he was, his enemies made sure of him.

But no.

Providence yet watched over him.

Another chance.

A bold chance of life.

Before his purpose could be divined, he plunged his spurs deeply into the reeking sides of his charger.

The horse rose in the air.

With one bound it had cleared the parapet of the bridge.

In another instant it was swimming calmly towards the bank with its rider, whom it had borne out of danger.

Several shots were fired at Titchbourne, but he landed in safety.

This gallant action so raised Chidiock in the estimation of his followers, that they welcomed him with the utmost enthusiasm, and rallying round him, fought with such vigour that they drove their opponents over the bridge, and compelled them to flee towards the town.

CHAPTER X.

BLACK TOWERS.

OF THE MANNER IN WHICH THE CONSPIRATORS CONTINUED THEIR MARCH—OF THE ILL-LUCK THAT SEEMED TO ACCOMPANY—AND OF THE NARROW ESCAPE OF CHIDIOCK TITCHBOURNE.

THE leading conspirators now commenced to muster their men.

They found that their actual loss was less than they expected, though several were severely wounded.

These were speedily attended to.

Those who had come out of the skirmish safely at once proceeded to put the castle into a state of defence.

"So far," cried Ballard, "all has gone well; the first battle has been won."

"True," was the reply of Chidiock Titchbourne, "but we cannot, must not tarry here."

"Why not?"

"Because the castle cannot hold out against a prolonged attack."

"Are we strong enough to march to Tutbury, and there seize the person of Mary, Queen of Scots?" boldly asked Thomas Salisbury.

"That were, indeed, a glorious idea, my son,' said John Ballard, clasping his hands in rapture; "the sacred person would, indeed, be a prize; with her amongst us, our success would become certain."

"I would wager a rose noble," said Robert Gage, "that long ere this, aye, upon the first notice of our rising, the wary Sir Amias Paulet has removed her to a place of greater security than the ruined fortress of Tutbury."

"Even if she were there," said John Travers, "we should have the whole garrison down upon us No—no; it would never do to attempt that."

"Nothing venture nothing have," cried John Ballard. "This is no time for childish hesitation; one bold stroke will paralyze our enemies, and make us masters of the position."

"True! Father Ballard is right," John Gage hastened to observe; "At all hazards we should rescue Queen Mary."

"Aye, my son; we should be ready to run any risk to have our Royal mistress amongst us."

Thus spoke Ballard.

"You know me too well, good Father Ballard," said Chidiock Titchbourne, "to doubt my readiness to undertake any project, however hazardous, which would offer even the remotest chance of success."

"Do you doubt the feasibility of this, then?" asked the priest.

"I do," was the reply. "In short, I cannot see the least hope of success, unless, indeed, our object could be gained by stratagem."

"Ho! stratagem?"

"Yes. First let us ascertain what support we can obtain, and then let us hasten to decide upon the measures to be adopted."

"I am content," cried old Captain Abington; "Titchbourne is right, though for my part I despair of success."

Though all the conspirators spoke boldly and bravely, still the hearts of all the leaders were rent by a secret misgiving.

For, that afternoon, when they repaired to the courtyard and assembled the men, they found that thirty-five men did not answer to their names.

Of this number more than half had been slain.

The others had disappeared.

The conspirators knew what had become of them.

They had deserted.

Whatever effect this scrutiny had upon the leaders of the conspiracy—

However terrible their forebodings, they still maintained a cheerful and confident demeanour.

Ballard harrangued the band in energetic and powerfully-exciting terms.

Raising his hand high above his head, he exposed to view a small figure of the Virgin.

He assured these conspirators that they were under the special protection of Heaven, whose cause they were then fighting.

Then, in loud and solemn tones, he recited a prayer for success and prosperity to their cause.

This was repeated aloud by the whole band.

The priest then pronounced a blessing upon all assembled, and once more they prepared to renew their march towards Tutbury.

The rain fell in torrents.

The roads were ploughed up with great ruts.

The band found it difficult to march in order.

They turned into the fields whenever it was practicable.

Under the most disheartening circumstances was their march continued.

This had a visible effect upon their men, and long ere they reached Tutbury, their force was still further diminished by the loss of a dozen more men.

Disheartened and depressed, the whole affair seemed to wear so unpromising an aspect that Titchbourne and Abington thought it prudent to seek the shelter of a huge barn which they came across, and then and there seek council of their friends.

"The men are disaffected, cold, wet and hungry," cried Titchbourne. "One by one they are leaving the ranks, and deserting the cause to which they have pledged themselves."

"What are we to do?"

"We can do nothing," said Thomas Salisbury, "but even if they all desert us, do we not remain "—

"We do! we do!"

"For my part," went on Titchbourne, "I am resolved to fight it out. I have sworn to continue my march as long as I can get a man to follow me, and when they are all gone, then I will conclude my journey alone. But I will never yield."

"We will all die together," cried Robert Gage. "There is now no retreat for us. It is either death upon the battle field or the scaffold."

"The former be my fate," cried Chidiock.

"And mine likewise," repeated the other.

The conspirators were determined to halt for the night at Black Towers, the family seat of Thomas Winter, which place they would have to pass on their road to Tutbury.

This idea was at once carried into effect, and ere nightfall, the conspirators were safely housed, and busy in seeing the requirements of their followers attended to.

A few hours repose, and the good fare afforded by the larders of Black Towers, effected so great a change, that the spirits of all revived, and to a very great extent confidence was once more restored.

A night of no small anxiety was passed by the leaders of the company.

Many a plan was proposed only to be rejected.

It had been arranged among them that they should in succession make the round of the place, in order to see that the sentinels were at their posts.

To these latter, strict orders had been given to fire upon any of their comrades who might attempt to desert.

Chidiock took upon himself the greater part of this duty.

An hour after midnight, Titchbourne was returning towards the house, after having visited the last outpost.

It was profoundly dark.

Advancing a few steps, our hero encountered a man.

Repressing the exclamation which rose to his lips, Titchbourne drew a petronel from his belt.

"Is that you, Captain Abington," asked a voice, which, brave as he was, Titchbourne recognised with a thrill of astonished terror.

It was the voice of Iscariot the renegade priest.

"Aye, 'tis I," muttered Titchbourne in a low tone, mimicking the gruff voice of the old captain.

"We must manage this better than we did the affair in Red Lion Court," pursued Iscariot. "Do you think that we can venture to surprise them now?"

"Hush, speak lower," whispered Titchbourne, grasping the priest by the arm, and leading him further down the garden. "Come this way, there is a sentinel within a few paces of us."

Iscariot did as he was bid, then he repeated his question.

"Can we not surprise them to-night?"

"I see no objection," cautiously replied Chidiock.

"Or shall we await the arrival of Sir William Fitzroy, the under sheriff of Staffordshire, and the yeomanry who are under arms."

"When will they arrive," queried Titchbourne, scarcely able to conceal the terrible anxiety which oppressed him.

"He cannot arrive here before daybreak, if so soon," returned Iscariot, and then we shall have to besiege the mansion.

"True."

Unfortunately in the skirmish some of the conspirators will most assuredly fall," went on Iscariot malignantly. "But I would not that harm should befal either John Ballard or Titchbourne, they must be captured alive, and share the tortures and fate of their leader Anthony Babington.

"I think that I can contrive their capture," observed Chidiock, "but the utmost caution must be used. I will return to the house, and having left the door open, will rejoin you here; in the meantime, assemble our men, if we can once secure the person of the chief conspirators, the rest will be easy, and the conspiracy will be at an end."

"You will run great risk, Captain Abington," remarked Iscariot, with affected concern.

"Heed me not," was the reply of the sham captain; "In a few minutes I will return. Get the men together as noiselessly as you can."

With this last observation Chidiock Titchbourne hastily withdrew.

Entering the house, he aroused his companions, and, instantly ordering the false traitor, Captain Abington (whom, it will be remembered, was the means of introducing Iscariot into the club in Red Lion Court), into custody, related the adventure that had befallen him.

"We must make Iscariot a prisoner," said Titchbourne, "for from him we shall be able to obtain much useful information."

"If those who accompany him offer the slightest resistance," said Ballard, firmly, "they must be put to death."

"What force have they?" asked Thomas Salisbury, with great uneasiness.

"I cannot judge precisely," replied Chidiock; "their numbers must be but few, since they are awaiting the arrival of Sir William Fitzroy."

"I know not what will be the issue of this," said Robert Gage, "but I am filled with apprehension."

"None of us, I am certain," remarked Charles Tilney, "are free from dark and gloomy presentiments, but we must cast them aside. Let us hasten and prepare for our foes."

Chidiock grasped his friend by the hand.

"Tilney is correct," he said; "come, let us hasten, for we have no time to lose."

Titchbourne then proceeded to call up the trustiest of his men.

Bidding them to observe the strictest silence, he placed them in various situations, so that they might appear instantaneously upon a given signal.

Then he returned to the garden, and coughed aloud.

He was answered by the advancing footsteps of two persons.

A voice demanded—

"Are you there, Captain Abington?"

Chidiock replied in the affirmative.

"Come nearer, then," rejoined Iscariot.

Titchbourne did so.

Suddenly there was a rush of men towards the spot.

Chidiock was seized.

A lantern was unmasked by one of his assailants, whom he recognised as Gifford.

The light fell full upon the face of our hero.

"Ha! ha!" laughed Iscariot; "you are caught in your own trap, Chidiock Titchbourne. You are my prisoner."

"Not so, villain."

And, by a powerful effort, Chidiock threw his assailants off.

Springing back, he drew his sword, and, making the blade describe a circle round his body, effected his retreat in safety.

A dozen shots were fired at him, but none hit him.

With a wild shout of defiance, he leaped the garden wall, and hastened towards the building.

CHAPTER XI.

THE CLOSE OF THE CONSPIRACY.

SHOWING HOW THE CONSPIRATORS WERE ATTACKED, AND OF THE TERRIBLE MANNER IN WHICH THEY WERE UTTERLY ROUTED.

ONCE more surrounded by part of the band, Titchbourne immediately placed himself at their head, and started in pursuit, but the Royalists had taken the alarm, and had fled.

Elated with his success, Chidiock Titchbourne returned to the house, and, giving each man a horn of strong ale, proposed, as a pledge, the "Restoration of the Church of Rome."

"We shall be speedily attacked again, my sons," said John Ballard; "it behoves us to be upon the alert."

Titchbourne proceeded to the courtyard and saw that all the defences were secure; that the drawbridge was raised, the sentinels at their posts, and everything prepared for the expected attack.

That day passed, still the enemy made no sign. The next night was dark, and the gloom was rendered yet more profound by a dense fog which prevailed.

All felt certain that the attack would take place this night.

Titchbourne walked round the moat.

He fancied that he heard stealthy footsteps upon the other side of the moat.

Listening intently, he found that he was not deceived; a large party of men were evidently making preparations to cross.

With a shout, Chidiock assembled his companions, who, at the expected signal, all sprang to arms, and stationed themselves at the exposed points.

The troopers had now advanced to within a hundred yards of the mansion.

The Royalists were headed by Sir William Fitzroy.

Immediately behind them was Gifford and Iscariot.

A trumpet then sounded, and a proclamation was read in a loud voice by a trooper, commanding the rebels, in the Queen's name, to surrender and deliver up their leaders.

Hardly had the unfortunate man finished, when a bullet from the petronel of Robert Gage laid him lifeless.

A shout of vindictive rage was raised by the Royalists.

The attack instantly commenced.

Several planks were thrown across the moat, and in spite of the efforts of the conspirators, many of their assailants succeeded in effecting a passage.

The conspirators fought bravely—all displayed equal courage—and equal disregard to danger.

Upon both sides a well directed fire was kept up.

The advantage lay with the conspirators.

The royalists were evidently wavering.

This gave them still greater hopes, and the rebels fought with renewed ardour.

However, fate was against them.

Their attention was called to another and a more terrible enemy.

From that moment the day was lost.

Fire! Fire! Fire!

The royalists had fired an out-building.

Efforts were made to extinguish the conflagration.

But without success.

Disaster followed disaster.

A second party of the royalists had crossed the moat, and had effected an entrance into the courtyard.

Titchbourne now perceived that the day was inevitably lost.

Putting himself at the head of a few faithful followers, Chidiock Titchbourne fought with all the fury of despair.

One by one his companions were shot down by his side.

Sir William Fitzroy saw that it would be useless to try and capture him without maiming him in some way.

He gave orders to them near him to that effect, at the same time admonishing the marksman, whom he had chosen for the work, not to slay him.

The man complied with this request.

Raising his petronel, he fired, and succeeded in hitting our hero just below the knee, crushing the cap.

With a low moan of agony, and a feeble attempt to deal a last blow at Iscariot, who advanced towards him, Chidiock Titchbourne fell back in a swooning state.

The conflict was now at an end; those few who continued struggling after their leaders had fallen, were speedily disarmed and bound.

Others who had made their escape into the fields, were pursued and recaptured.

The whole of the prisoners were then securely lodged in the dungeons of the Black Towers, and the following morning commenced their journey to the Tower of London.

The Babington Conspiracy was at an end.

CHAPTER XII

SHOWING THE WAY IN WHICH THE CONSPIRA-
TORS MET THEIR DEATH, AND OF CHIDIOCK
TITCHBOURNE'S LAST FAREWELL.

THE plot had failed.

The whole of the conspirators were speedily captured, and so great was the terror of Elizabeth's government that no time was lost in bringing them to trial.

During its progress it was plainly shown how the leaders of the conspiracy had been practised on by the subtlety of the Priest Ballard.

In fact, Camden mentions Ballard as a "disguised Jesuit of great intrepidity and talent—a silken priest in a soldier's habit."

Versatile intriguer, as he was—assuming all names and disguises, as he did—with all the wondrous art and cunning knowledge of a political Jesuit, ye yet found himself entrapped in the nets of crafty Walsingham.

"Oh, Ballard! Ballard!" the judge who presided could not refrain from exclaiming; "Oh, Ballard! what hast thou done a sort (a company) of brave youths, otherwise endued with good gifts, whom, by thy inducements, thou hast brought to their utter destruction and confusion!"

In answer, the priest, who felt some compunction at the tragical executions which were to follow, replied—

"That he wished that all the blame might rest upon him, could the shedding of his blood be the saving of the other's lives?"

In the progress of the trial, the history and feelings of many of those engaged in the conspiracy appears.

The most pathetic instances of romantic friendship occurred.

One had engaged in the plot to serve his friend, for he had no hopes of it, nor any wish of its success; he had observed to his friend, that the haughty and ambitious mind of Anthony Babington would be the destruction of himself and his friend, nevertheless he was willing to die with them.

Donne, who before the conspiracy had given up housekeeping, said——

"I called back my servants again together, and began to keep house again more freshly than ever, I did it only because I was weary to see Tom Salisbury, the best man in my country, of whom I only made choice, or else break my allegiance to my sovereign and undo myself and posterity for ever."

Charles Tilney said——

"In flying away with my friend, I fulfilled the part of a friend."

The Judge remarked——

"Oh, Tilney, to perform your friendship, you have broken your allegiance to your sovereign."

Charles Tilney seemed deeply grieved at this rebuke, and bowed his head remarking——

"Therein I have offended."

Robert Gage was questioned as to his reason for flying into the woods, where he was found with some of the conspirators, and he replied, tenderly looking round to his unfortunate friends——

"For company."

The time now came for the sentence of condemnation to be passed.

Every heart in the court felt for the noble band, whose ultimate end was clear to every one.

The noble nature of these gentlemen did not recoil from the most fearful and barbarous of deaths.

Their sole aim being that those near and dear to them, should not suffer through their folly.

The day of execution came, and they were removed from the Tower to Lincoln's Inn Fields, to pay the penalty of the law.

The process of execution was of the most barbarous character, and revolting to the social feelings of the culprits, being a scene most ghastly and full of horrors.

The open space in front of the place of execution was crowded by sightseers, the majority consisting of the worst characters, and there were not a few lazy apprentices.

Ballard was first partly executed, and snatched alive from the gallows to be disembowelled.

Titchbourne looked on with undaunted countenance, steadily gazing on the horrible tortures which he in a moment was to pass through. He had left wife, children, sisters, and a domestic hearth, that was dear to him to enter into the conspiracy, and therefore when his time came, he was constrained to breathe softly, "friendship hath brought me to this."

When the end of Ballard was announced Titchbourne's executioner advanced, but the crowd who felt a sympathy for him, called upon him to speak.

He advanced, and thus addressed the assemblage:

"Countrymen, and my dear friends, you expect that I should speak something.

"I am a bad orator, and my text is worse.

CHIDIOCK TITCHBOURNE.

"It were in vain to enter into the discourse of the whole matter for which I am brought hither, for that it hath been revealed heretofore.

"Let me be a warning to all young gentlemen, especially those generous in friendship.

"I had a friend, a dear friend, of whom I made no small account, whose friendship hath brought me to this, he told me the whole matter. I cannot deny as they had laid it down to be done, but I always thought it impious and denied to be a dealer in it.

"Before this chanced, I lived together in most flourishing estate. Of whom went report in the Strand, Fleet Street and elsewhere about London, but Titchbourne and his friends?

"Thus I lived, and wanted nothing I could wish for, and God knows what was less in my head than matters of State.

Now, give me leave to declare the miseries I sustained after I was acquainted with the action, wherein I may justly compare my state to that of Adam, who could not abstain from one forbidden thing to enjoy all other things the world could afford. The terror of conscience awaited me.

"After I considered the dangers whereunto I was fallen, I went to Sir John Peters, in Essex, and appointed my horses should meet me in London, intending to go down into the country.

"I came to London, and then heard that all was betrayed, whereupon, like Adam, we fled into the wood to hide ourselves.

"My dear countrymen, my sorrows may be your joy, yet mix your smiles with tears, and pity my case.

I am descended from a house two hundred years before the Conquest, never stained till this, my misfortune.

"I have a wife and one child; my wife Agnes, my dear wife—and there's my grief—and six sisters left in my hands. My poor servants! I know, their master being taken, were dispersed, for all of which I do most heartily grieve. I expected some favour, though I deserved nothing less—that the remainder of my years might have recompensed my former guilt, which, seeing I have missed, let me now meditate on the joys I hope to enjoy."

Titchbourne now took his place and prepared for his doom. Although in his last speech he had become somewhat nervous, coolness never forsook him, and in the midst of his agonies he cried out—

Parce mihi, Domine Jesu.
("Spare me, Lord Jesus.")

On the night previous to this Tichborne wrote a most tender and loving letter to his dear wife the original of which is now preserved in the Harleian MSS. in the British Museum.

Our story has drawn to a close, and, trusting that we have been successful in pourtraying, under a guise of a romance, a truthful and authentic narrative of this *remarkable* conspiracy, we take a farewell of the gentle reader, and hope to receive from his hands a favourable verdict for

TRAITORS' GATE.

THE BRITISH LIBRARY!

CONTAINING

The most Powerful, Original and Complete Stories ever Written.

All by British Authors! No American Reprints!! Illustrated!!!

No. 1.—DEADLY NIGHTSHADE; a Story of London SHADY SOCIETY!

No. 2.—THE DEATH WATCH; Or, the DOOM OF DARVIL!
32 Pages, with Coloured Wrapper, and Engravings. Price TWOPENCE.

No. 3.—THE TRAITORS' GATE; a Story of the TOWER OF LONDON,

A Splendid Historical Romance, by the Author of DEADLY NIGHTSHADE. 32 Pages, with Coloured Wrapper, and Engravings. Price Two PENCE.
Now in preparation

No. 4.—RAYMOND the RED HAND; Or, OUTCAST FROM THE WORLD!

32 Pages, with Coloured Wrapper, and Engravings. This Splendid Romance will be found to equal if not excel in Interest and Power, those of DUMAS or EUGENE SUE. Price TWOPENCE. Others will follow very shortly.

Published by G. HOWE, 7, Red Lion-ct., Fleet-st., London, & all Booksellers.

NOW PUBLISHING

RE-ISSUE of TYBURN TREE;

OR, THE HIGHWAYMEN OF ENGLAND!

No. 1 commenced with the Novel and Exciting Career of

GALLOPING DICK and SLIPPERY JACK! the Boy Highwaymen.

Nos. 1 and 2 together, in Coloured Wrapper, Price ONE PENNY.

In No. 10 is commenced the only true and authentic Life of

JACK SHEPPARD and his Friend BLUESKIN (Jolly Nose)

To be followed by

The Life of DICK TURPIN; CLAUDE DUVAL; SIXTEEN-STRING JACK; BOLD BRENNAN; and in fact all the Daring Highwaymen, &c., who expiated their Crimes on Tyburn Tree.

LIST OF PRIZES with No. 1. PRIZE CHEQUE with No. 3. PICTURES (gratis) with Nos. 4 and 9. Others in preparation. Price ONE PENNY (Weekly.)

THE

INTERNATIONAL HERALD,

A NEWSPAPER for the PEOPLE, is published every Thursday, Price ONE PENNY.
GEO. HOWE, 7, Red Lion Court, Fleet Street, London.

AUSTRALIAN MEAT

AND

AMERICAN PRESERVED PROVISIONS.

How to Cook, Eat, and Enjoy in 80 different ways. This Useful Work is highly commended by the Press, and should be in the hands of every Lady in the Land, and of all interested in reducing the price of Butcher's Meat.
GEO. HOWE, 7, Red Lion Court, Fleet Street, London.